MW01241165

Kaity's Catch

J.J. Sommers

Fox Folk Press

Copyright © 2022 by J.J. Sommers

All rights reserved. No part of this publication may be reproduced, stored or transmitted in any form or by any means, electronic, mechanical, photocopying, recording, scanning, or otherwise without written permission from the publisher. It is illegal to copy this book, post it to a website, or distribute it by any other means without permission.

This novel is entirely a work of fiction. The names, characters and incidents portrayed in it are the work of the author's imagination. Any resemblance to actual persons, living or dead, events or localities is entirely coincidental.

Cover by Fiona Jayde of FionaJaydeMedia.com

Editing by Donna A. Martz of MartzProofing.com

Contents

Also by J.J. Sommers

For more pole dance romance and for sneak peeks, please subscribe to my newsletter:
http://jjsommerswrites.com

Chapter 1

K aity paused at the pole dance studio's door, nervously slid her phone out of her purse, and slid it back in. Curtains obscured her view inside, but she could see the studio's logo on the door: a straight line topped with a stylized snapdragon flower, and below the snapdragon, sparse curlicues that suggested a woman's form at the base of the pole.

Like the woman is growing into a flower, Kaity thought, and then blushed, because it was a dumb thing to think. And her husband hadn't been afraid to tell her so whenever she opened her mouth to say these things out loud. Ex-husband, she mentally corrected herself.

"Kaity!" Anabelle rushed up, waving her car keys and wearing her usual grin. Relieved, Kaity hugged her friend and stopped fiddling with her phone.

"Sorry I'm late, traffic sucked as usual," Anabelle said.

"It's okay, I was just, um…looking." The words sounded stupid as soon as they left her lips, which was sadly common in Kaity's life.

"Well, I got our tickets to the showcase so we're good to go! Oh, I know, let's grab a quick selfie for the group chat."

Kaity forced a smile as Anabelle tugged her in, snapped a picture, and then sent it to the Divorced Ladyfriends group, who'd been her lifeline these past few months. Then Kaity noticed that she was still clutching her phone with one hand, forced herself to relax, and opened the door for them.

Anabelle jetted to the front desk to talk to the woman standing behind it while Kaity took it all in: the walls were uniformly a light magenta, more of a fuchsia, and the abstract logo appeared in multiple places. The front room was furnished like an office waiting room with low sofas and end tables, except with large framed photos of women in what Kaity assumed were various poses on the pole that one would learn at the studio. She wryly thought, my fat ass isn't staying up on a pole without duct tape.

"Come on," Anabelle said, "I've checked us in and we can find seats." She led them through a curtained doorway into a larger room, where dozens of folding chairs surrounded two poles in the center of the room.

"How much do I owe you for the tickets?" Kaity asked as they navigated past women also in their 30s, plus some older and younger women, and a couple of visibly uncomfortable men.

"Nah, I've got it," said Anabelle. "I know your divorce just went through. And besides, I was hoping you'd enjoy the performance enough to take classes! It looks really fun!"

Kaity felt her hand reaching for her phone again: she wanted a distraction, any distraction, any reason to not be in the conversation. Her cheeks burned while she considered all the reasons she wanted to be anywhere but here.

"I, uh, work has been busy—"

Anabelle playfully slapped her hand. "Oh, stop! You work nine-to-five just like me! And I needed to get out of the house and be distracted after my divorce, so I figured you'd be the same way! "

Unlikely, Kaity reflected glumly. True, she and Anabelle were both in their mid-30s, both divorced, and they'd met in a MeetUp group for divorced women looking to make new friends. Some of them had bonded, facetiously naming themselves the "divorced ladyfriends" and starting a group chat. Anabelle was at the center of their social activities. But Anabelle was a smile on legs, one of those people who constantly looked happy, and seemed to actually be happy too. Kaity was mostly just anxious, a fact which her ex-husband had reminded her of often.

The lights flickered, and Kaity flashed Anabelle an apologetic smile. Maybe there was still some way for her to wiggle out of this. The divorce had been amicable, so no need for expensive lawyers, but she could still claim that times were lean. She'd had to get her own place and decorate it, after all. And while apartments didn't ultimately cost that much in the Midwest...

Moments later, the lights dimmed, and Kaity tried to shut off her brain so she could enjoy the show, not that she knew anything about pole dancing.

A woman emerged from a break within the chairs and walked to the spotlighted place between the two poles. Kaity automatically cataloged her appearance: probably around her same height, five-five or five-six, younger (mid 20s?), also white, blond, with a smile to rival Anabelle's, and slim with cheekbones and musculature that popped under the harsh lighting. Her muscles, Kaity noted enviously, were easily visible because she wore black short-shorts with suspenders fitted over an adorable white crop top with a snappy little collar, blending business and play.

"Welcome to the Snapdragon spring showcase!" she beamed into the mic she held. Her voice showed her youth, yes, but in the back of her mind Kaity found herself wondering if this woman would do vocal work for her instructional design company, because having a compelling narrator could make all the difference between a successful and a failed module.

"Most of you know me, I'm Jenny, founder and owner of Snapdragon. I'll be your MC tonight, as we watch our students and instructors perform in a variety of pole and related genres." There was more than one pole dance thing out there? Kaity shuddered; her main memory of pole dance was John taking her out to a strip club one time, to "spice up their marriage." Her ex-husband's running commentary on every woman's body, comparing them to her own, had tainted the experience. It was hard enough for Kaity not to compare her body to those of other women, and just remembering the strip club experience made her want to curl in on herself with shame.

Jenny went on to describe some of the differences between trick-oriented pole and low flow and chair dancing and twerking, which might or might not involve a pole. Kaity stopped clenching her phone for a moment to brush her brown hair out of her eyes; she'd taking to wearing it down lately to try to avoid giving the impression that she was as uptight as John had accused her of being.

"...so, first up, we have one of our Snapdragon instructors, Sophia! Sophia likes to sizzle and snap, and what you're about to see is her competition choreography that won first place last fall!"

There are pole dance competitions? Kaity wondered, and then her thoughts ground to a halt when the lights dimmed, Jenny stepped back into the darkness, and in the next moment, a cloaked body crawled into the center of the floor, then knelt in a tightly curled-up position, their figure still completely obscured.

Rusty music box sounds filled the room, a little creepy and definitely not sexy. Kaity relaxed when she picked up on the tune: this was a cover of "Come Little Children" from a witchy movie. As the song ticked on for a few more moments, the cloaked figure remained still, and Kaity found herself leaning in a little, wondering what would happen next.

A hand shot out from the cloak, making an alluring, come-hither motion to the audience. Then it retreated. Next, a foot emerged, shod in a black leather ankle-high boot. Suddenly, the cloak was whisked off and the bikini-clad body underneath flipped—all while the perfectly-pointed foot remained extended—and the dancer sprang from a prone position into the splits. Kaity felt herself audibly gasp.

Over the duration of the song, Sophia climbed the pole, fell into the splits, got herself upside down, did the splits again while on the pole, and completed a variety of other movements that Kaity could not have described in any detail beyond slinky, strong, and wow. Sophia wore a confident smirk the entire time, languidly reaching down in resting moments to brush her red hair from her face or trail a hand down a bare thigh while in one of her many splits poses.

One of the women sitting in the row behind Kaity murmured reverently, "She's got the strongest shoulder mount I've ever seen." Not that Kaity knew what a shoulder mount was, but the tone sounded about right for what she was seeing.

The song ended, and Kaity felt herself take a deep breath, one she hadn't realized that she'd been holding. For one brief, aching moment, she wondered what it would feel like to be as sexy and confident as Sophia had been on stage, to actually *feel* that way and not fake it, not have her self-esteem crumbling like a forlorn sandcastle. Not hate her image in the mirror. Nor her body trying on clothes. What would it take?

Jenny returned to announce the next performer, and the next. The following eight to ten acts passed in a blur of bodysuits and booty shorts. While Sophia's routine had drawn Kaity in and blown her mind, the rest were a mix of fun, sexy, and funny dances. The diversity of bodies and ages was pretty impressive too; more than one dancer had silver hair. Kaity found herself cringing when seeing women curvier than her in revealing outfits, and then she mentally berated herself for being so judgmental. As the intermission drew near, Kaity put a positive spin on it, wondering if any of the dancers modeled for stock images, as she always needed more diverse bodies to use in modules for work.

After an aggressive dance with heel clacks—loud sounds when the dancer's shoes' toe boxes collided with the floor or each other—that made Kaity start in her seat, intermission was called. Anabelle turned to Kaity with an expectant smile on her face.

"What did you think?"

Kaity tried on a smile in return. "It was neat. I've never really seen anything like it before."

"What was your favorite act?"

"Sophia, for sure," Kaity said. "The way she moved..." she paused for a moment, not sure how to finish the sentence. *Like she doesn't hate herself? Like she actually likes who she is? Like she feels confident and sexy at the same time?*

Anabelle leaned in conspiratorially. "I know what you mean. Everyone wants to move like her. Which is why it's good she teaches here, right? Like maybe we could take classes with her?"

Kaity scowled. "You're just trying to trap me into taking classes with you." It had become a running joke in their divorced ladyfriends group that Anabelle's hobbies eventually became everyone's hobbies.

"No, really! There's a seven-week session for beginners coming up, and I just know you'd love it—"

"I'll think about it," Kaity cut her off, standing to end the conversation. "I'm going to find the bathroom." There's no way she'd take a pole dance class and be totally humiliated by showing up to something wearing booty shorts and being completely incompetent at the same time. Confidence was a good goal, but it could wait...like it always did.

Chapter 2

G abe knelt to swap out a lens, snapped a few sample shots, and then stood up just in time to catch Jenny walking into the green room with all the swagger of a circus ringleader. She struck a pose, and he captured her infectious smile.

"Show's off to a great start. Sophia is killing it with her showcase routine," Jenny reported.

Gabe nodded, turned to snap another few candids of other dancers waiting their turn, and returned his focus to Jenny.

"I'm sure she's rocking it, the pics I got during the rehearsal were amazing," he replied. Learning to shoot dance was a totally different endeavor from weddings, his main gig, and it was a challenge he was enjoying.

Jenny—as tall as he was in her heels—peered over his shoulder and said, "Oops, I have to go reassure some first-time performers. I'll be around!" He nodded again, then continued to alternate between fiddling with his camera settings and capturing candid shots of the dancers waiting their turn.

Sophia breezed in, Jenny flitted out, and the show went on. Gabe took pictures of the studio's performers, from newer students to seasoned artists, as they struck both serious and silly poses. The twerk team got into handstands against the wall for him to shoot, while another performer captured their twerking on her phone. A pair of friends, one towering over the other in her eight-inch heels, hugged each other while making bunny ears behind each other's heads. Another woman, dressed as an actual bunny since she'd been performing a seasonally fitting naughty Easter Bunny dance, photo-bombed them within a few moments. Since Jenny had brought Gabe in as the informal studio photographer at the previous showcase, everyone was familiar and friendly with Gabe's presence, even as Snapdragon was primarily a women's space.

Not that I mind one bit, Gabe thought to himself, setting down his camera to run a hand through his hair. A studio full of gorgeous women ready to collaborate on artistic shoots? Meeting Jenny at the local entrepreneurs' lunch had been a godsend. It wouldn't generate enough business to get him out of the soul-sucking wedding industry, but it would give him something artsy to look forward to.

If he was being honest with himself, he mused as a dancer painted like a tiger in a tiger-striped sports bra and shorts set posed for him, he was in a good place with his career. There was no shortage of weddings to cover, but there was also no one to help him celebrate his wins. Not that he was eager to be tied down like in some of the more painful relationships he'd observed, which he'd had front-row seats to while watching their mutual self-destruction.

The tiger-striped dancer, Lydia, curled her fingers in like a cat's paw to strike another cheeky pose. She was cute, but married, and he also didn't tend to look for partners where he worked. If something happened, it happened, but he had to protect his reputation in order to keep getting cool gigs like the one he was currently at; nobody wanted a male photographer who turned out to be perving on all the women at a shoot. It helped that Snapdragon had three dance spaces, with the performers' changing area in the room behind him, and the performance area in the room ahead of him and the green room serving as a buffer between the two.

Not that the division seemed to matter, he reflected wryly, noticing a pair of performers helping each other unbuckle and refasten some kind of garter things on their shorts.

"Intermission after this next act!" Jenny's voice rang out.

Gabe slung his camera strap over his neck and decided to hit the bathroom before the deluge of people would head the same direction. He'd already taken photos of each routine during the dress rehearsal; tonight was all about snapping the candid pics and capturing the festive mood the performers were in. It was a fun night out and once he'd released the amount of photos he and Jenny had negotiated, he could charge his normal rate for edits, which would bring in a nice bit of money...and to think, his family had never approved of his artistic choice in careers. And yet here he was, surrounded by beautiful women who were also artists at the top of their game. What more could he want?

Chapter 3

Kaity easily found the two doors of the restroom in the main lobby, and luckily the initial rush from when intermission was called seemed to have died down. As she plucked her phone from her purse to scroll through whatever was happening, she heard one of the doors unlatch, and she started towards it.

Face buried in her phone, she bumped into someone's chest. She looked up.

The chest belonged to a person a head taller than her, with nice brown eyes and curly brown hair. The eyes were opened wide in hostile surprise, and it took Kaity a second to realize why: if he hadn't been quick enough to snatch his camera out of the way, she would've smashed straight into it.

"Um, sorry," she said quickly. Shame burned up her face. Was she ever *not* a screw-up?

He spared a glance for his camera, then looked back at her. "It's okay," he said, and his face thawed out to a pleasant, neutral expression. He'd put out his other hand to steady her, and Kaity felt the warmth through her thin cardigan. It felt nice.

Realizing that she was still standing inches away from his chest, Kaity tried to step around him. He stepped in the same direction. They both laughed nervously. Or, at least Kaity laughed nervously; the man's laugh seemed natural and not forced.

"Go ahead," the man said, extending an arm to point the way and smoothly stepping to the other side. Kaity ducked into the bathroom, trying to calm the interior voice that loved to go through the list of all her mistakes. Breaking the studio photographer's camera would be a really nice addition to the list, and a good reason for her to never come back here again...so maybe her clumsiness now would've spared her future embarrassment. She would never know. She tried to shake the critical mood as she washed her hands and got ready to return to her seat.

Gabe returned to the green room. There were more beautiful women to photograph, but he found himself thinking about the one he'd just literally bumped into. He hadn't seen her at the studio before, and she definitely wasn't one of the performers, so it was likely that she was someone's friend or family member. Or maybe just a pole hobbyist, someone who took classes once a week here or at another studio in town and then turned up to watch the showcase. With her dark brown, slightly wavy hair and rounded cheeks, Gave could picture her fitting right into a pre-Raphaelite painting, in a sheer gauzy gown that, if he continued to think about it, would undoubtedly distract him from doing his job.

Jenny flew in and out of the green room on her heels, helping with hairspray and velcro issues alike. Gabe captured the small moments: one dancer's look of concentration with a bobby pin clenched between teeth, another's graceful forward fold to rub sticky gel on her ankles, and an embrace as two friends whispered affirmations in each other's ears right before going on stage to nail a particularly difficult doubles routine.

As the final acts went on, Gabe found a folding chair and went to have a seat. He looked over some of the photos, already getting a sense for which ones he liked. He didn't know enough about pole to understand which moves were more difficult than others, but he was good at making the dancers look good, and that's why they kept bringing him back.

If there was one thing Gabe knew, it was that he was good at what he did. Even if his family didn't approve. Even if choosing his career had meant making other sacrifices. His lips tightened with old memories.

Moments after Jenny strode in to announce the final bow, Gabe felt his phone buzz. He reached into his pocket to lift it out and glanced at it.

Seeing red was not an accurate description for how he felt when he saw the text. Not with his highly trained eye.

It was more of a white-out, a rage and sadness that fuzzed the edges of his vision while he dismissed the text and forced himself not to think about its implications.

He didn't need *her* bullshit right now, and he wouldn't let it ruin an otherwise fun work engagement.

But just in case, he texted Alex: *Bro, potential for a rough night. Want to meet up for a beer?*

Kaity joined Anabelle and the rest of the audience in a standing ovation as the dancers all ushered in for their final bow. Flushed, happy faces beamed back at the audience, and Kaity felt her lips tug up into a smile to match. Maybe coming here hadn't been a mistake; she'd gotten out of her apartment, hung out with a fellow divorced ladyfriend, and seen some cool dance. It was a little like watching the gymnasts in the Olympics, only with way more skin showing, and the potential for someone impaling themselves on a seven-inch heel.

She followed Anabelle into the lobby, enjoying the afterglow around her. Performers hugged their friends and family members, took silly selfies, and groaned as they stepped out of high heels, rolling their ankles and comparing bruises. From where they stood near the front desk, Kaity could see one of the silver-haired dancers posing with kids—her children? or maybe her grandchildren? —which made Kaity smile a tiny bit. Some people got to lead happy lives, it seemed. The more people-watching she did, the more tender moments she noticed.

As a result, Kaity didn't realize that Anabelle was signing them both up for the beginner class until she was asked for her credit card.

"Um, when is this again?" she asked, trying to catch up.

"Mondays from six to seven pm," Anabelle said, in that I-am-just-reminding-you-since-you-al-ready-agreed-to-this voice she tended to bust out whenever a divorced ladyfriend was trying to back out of a growth opportunity, social opportunity, or better yet, both in one.

Kaity already had her phone in her hand, so she pulled up her calendar. Damn, Anabelle was right...there was nothing in her calendar beyond work. Except for a date three months from now, when things would finally get better.

"I'm in," she said, hoping she sounded firm and committed. Anabelle beamed and Jenny beamed and Kaity did her best impression of them. She handed over her card, signed a waiver, and put in a calendar notification for next Monday and the six subsequent Mondays.

"I'm so excited!" Anabelle gushed when they turned away from the desk. "I've been wanting to do this forever!" Her enthusiasm touched Kaity, and Kaity wondered if she could fake her way to Anabelle-levels of happiness. Maybe the calm confidence Sophia had exuded on the stage was only months away too. And maybe hell would freeze over.

Kaity spotted the photographer in the crowd by the front door and paused. She tugged on Anabelle's elbow. "He's cute, right? I ran into him by the bathroom, and I thought he seemed cute and nice." Anabelle gave him a once-over and nodded. "Very cute. You should ask him out."

"No way," Kaity replied. "I'm nowhere near ready to date again. Definitely feeling too screwed up still."

"It's been six months," Anabelle said. "You're totally ready! We can ask the group chat." Kaity shook her head vehemently. "Okay, just go ask for his number." Another head shake. "Or I will."

"You're terrible," Kaity berated her friend, though her lips tugged up to show that she didn't mean it. And that maybe she enjoyed having someone have her back for once. "I will just introduce myself, okay? Is that enough for you?" Anabelle, the ruthless encourager of their group, bounced up and down in agreement. Her blond hair, pixie-cut short, flopped in amiable timing.

Kaity wove through the crowd, dodging some impressively sweaty twerkers. A dancer in a leotard with star-shaped cut-outs bent over to remove her kneepads, and Kaity stopped before bumping into her. There may be hope for me on a pole yet, she thought.

She reached where Gabe was leaning against one of the studio walls, deep in his phone, and tossed a quick beseeching look back at Anabelle. Thumb-ups and a wild grin.

Kaity cleared her throat and said, "Hey, I'm Kaity. Sorry for bumping into you earlier."

He raised his head, and she got a glimpse of tawny eyes. But they were narrowed in...anger? Disgust? Hurt?

"Gabe. No worries." Kaity forced herself not to recoil at the curt tone. He glanced back down at his phone, then pocketed it and pushed off from the wall. "I've gotta go. See you around."

For the second time that day, Kaity's cheeks burned, and she walked back to where Anabelle was almost bouncing with excitement.

"How'd it go?!"

"Eh," Kaity said. "He seemed like he didn't want to talk to me." She hoped her voice didn't waver. "If I can't handle rejection at this stage, I'm probably not ready to date again."

"Nonsense!" Anabelle asserted. Her enthusiasm made Kaity smile, even if not much else could at that moment. "He probably just has a lot going on, having photographed backstage for the last two hours. If he's not the right guy for you, we'll find someone else." Then Anabelle linked arms with Kaity and they walked out of the studio, planning what to wear to the first day of their pole dance class. Kaity looked back at the studio over her shoulder. If she could find something to wear that made her feel one-eighth as confident as Sophia had looked in her dance, maybe things would be okay. And maybe she'd meet a nice guy who actually wanted to talk to her. Yeah, right.

Chapter 4

K aity grabbed a cardigan on her way out of the door; late springtime in the Midwest meant rising temperatures, but the office was often chilly. It was a quiet drive from her apartment in SoBro—local slang for South Broad River—to downtown, where she parked in the office parking structure and walked into the regional headquarters of InstructCo, the instructional design company where she'd worked for a number of years.

Phone clutched in one hand, she scanned her calendar: yes, two meetings today. She pulled her cardigan out from under the crook of her arm once she reached her desk and tried to tie it nicely around her shoulders. Like most of her work-wear, the dress she had on today had sleeves that went down to her elbows, and this dress happened to be a floral-print fabric with an A-line cut. It flattered her figure and hid most of the places where she was, in both her and her ex-husband's opinion, too curvy.

"Kaity?" Her boss, Antonio, popped his head into her office. She turned and smiled at him: slightly older, generally kind.

"Yes, what's up?"

"In addition to those two client meetings, I'm going to ask you to take a new hire around the office this morning."

"Oh, okay," Kaity replied. Something tugged at her memory—they were a small branch, not due for many new hires soon, unless this was someone's relative who needed a job out of college, maybe? —and then she turned back to her desktop to start setting up for the day.

She wrapped one hand around her ever-present travel mug, filled with her favorite loose-leaf tea from a shop back home in Louisville. Once she and John had moved here, she'd made sure to order their tea online, so she could always have a reminder of home. This was late March; they'd moved last July and gotten divorced three months later. John had not only a job here but also family, and Kaity had nothing, no one.

Immersing herself in work, she checked on the modules she was in charge of creating for their corporate clients, happy that her attention to detail seemed to be shining through and making everything look professional and nice. Working in learning technology hadn't been her first pick, but in college she had vacillated between becoming an historian and a librarian, and after contemplating and discarding the idea of grad school, she had ended up at this company in Louisville, then married to John, then asking for a transfer to the Mariontown office when he had wanted to move closer to his family.

The travel mug of tea got her through her first hour of emails and project details. As she drained the mug and rose to rinse it out, there was another knock at her open office door.

Antonio said through the door, already on his way to someone else's office, "Here's our new hire, can you help acclimate her and then drop her back off at my office?"

Kaity shouted "Sure!" through the door and was already crossing the small space to get from her desk to the door when she saw who stood in the door frame.

Blond hair fell to her shoulders in waves. Red lips and red nails both curved wickedly, showing who she was at her rotten core: a poison apple.

Her sister-in-law. *Ex*-sister-in-law. Betrayer.

Gabe pulled into the Broad River coffee shop's parking lot. It was around ten a.m, and there were plenty of seats available both outside and inside. Pairs and clusters of college students hunched over laptops, studying and completing group projects. A younger woman and an older woman had pushed two strollers together so the infants inside could have a staring contest while the adults sipped their lattes in oversized mugs.

Pausing to reflect gratefully on the perks of setting one's own hours, Gabe got himself a coffee and waited for Jenny to show up. As she also set her own hours outside of when the pole studio was open, she rolled in shortly after.

Blowing on her mug of herbal tea, Jenny joined Gabe at the table he'd selected, and they started looking over showcase photos. Jenny would know which ones were bloopers and had to be deleted before Gabe put them online for performers to purchase from him, and she would want to buy a few as well, to promote the studio. He gave her a good rate, and being able to shoot at the studio and sell to performers helped him grow his business, making it a win-win situation for them both.

After some time selecting photos, they leaned back and switched to chit-chat. They'd started off friendly and become friends at some point in the last few months, and so catching up was now normal once business was taken care of. Gabe was happy to have a friend in Jenny; she had a keen mind for both art and business, and her anatomical knowledge was spot-on (which had been very helpful when he'd needed advice for a muscle cramp after an intense day of a pre-wedding shoot).

"Was everything okay on the night of the showcase?" Jenny finally asked.

Gabe drained his mug of coffee and set it down too loudly, earning him a look from one of the college students.

"Yeah, I just..." he sighed. "My family is local. My stepmother and I don't get along. She picked that night to bother me."

"Do you want to talk about it?" Jenny asked.

"Not really. I want it to go away, but it won't."

In that moment, Gabe chose to steer the conversation in other directions.

"Any new students sign up after the showcase?"

Jenny's concerned look was replaced by a smile. "Yes! We always get a few. I'll have a full class of beginners on Monday nights, and even though the next showcase isn't for another few months, I'm thinking of creating some choreography classes just to get new people comfortable performing."

Gabe eased back into a smile. "Cool. I'll be there to photograph them once they're ready." To his relief, the conversation continued to flow naturally about work and business, until Jenny had to leave to open the studio for afternoon classes, and Gabe was left to his own devices, which most certainly did not include following up with any family members. Alex worked a nine-to-five but Gabe could always find some of his fellow artists to chat with, like Johnny B or Ian, since they rented studio space near Broad River. Or he could drop some more business cards around town. Or whatever he wanted, really.

He picked up his empty coffee mug, put it down again. Stared into it, trying to decide if he wanted more coffee or not. Of course that was a yes; he was an artist, after all.

The more Gabe fiddled with the photos, the more he realized that his schedule was too open. No weddings until the weekend, and it was only Monday. Maybe if he found an excuse to swing by Snapdragon, he'd run into that cute woman again...Katie? He'd been distracted by family BS but that was nothing new. And there was a good Mexican place by the studio anyway, so he could camp out there enjoying endless chips and queso while editing photos.

Georgia's smile was predatory. "Hey, Kaity. How do you like it here?"

Kaity noticed the inflection on "here," the way Georgia drew out the word and imbued it with meaning: "here," this office; "here," this job; "here," this city, unlike the other city where she'd lived when she had met John and they'd gotten married and then decided to move here.

And Kaity remembered, in an unpleasant moment that kept compounding, how before the divorce she'd offered to help Georgia get a job in instructional design, and had recommended her for an opening at her company. That had been months ago. Kaity had put it out of her mind, with so many other logistics to wrangle. The numbness from that time began to flood Kaity's senses, her mouth dry and tasting bitter.

And here Georgia was.

Lost in analyzing, lost in anxiety, it took Kaity a moment to cut through the fog and respond.

"It's great. I'm great. I'm supposed to show you around. Let's do that." Kaity lurched past Georgia and out of the door and into the hallway, giving a perfunctory tour while her mind screamed that this was wrong, this awful woman shouldn't be in her workplace.

Antonio came back to lead Georgia to a temporary office until she got her own set-up. Kaity sat back down at her desk, day effectively ruined.

Her phone pinged. Anabelle was texting: *Ready for the big day? Pole class tonight!!! <3*

Kaity put her head down on her desk. The surface was cool but not comforting. And she'd thought the day couldn't get any worse.

Chapter 5

5:30pm rolled around, and Kaity had already tried on and discarded three outfits. The informative email from Snapdragon had informed her that in the Pole Basics class, leggings or yoga pants were acceptable, or shorts if the dancer preferred. A sports bra with a camisole or T-shirt would work too. Beginning dancers usually danced barefoot, though they might wear leg warmers or socks until they had warmed up.

At last, Kaity selected a favorite pair of charcoal gray yoga pants, cropped above the ankle, and a matching sports bra. She pulled on a shirt she'd bought at a yoga boutique Anabelle had dragged her to last month; it was cream-colored, stretchy, and did a crisscross thing in the back that Kaity assumed did not conform to Euclidian geometry. She pulled her hair back in a ponytail and started the drive to the studio.

Once there, she waited in her car. She would spot Anabelle and they would walk in together and somehow it would be okay.

Her phone pinged. It was Anabelle again: *omg traffic running late D:*

Kaity, with monumental effort, got out of her car and started toward the studio. This will be fine, she told herself. No more bad surprises. No more terrible people.

She saw Gabe leaving the studio. He held the door open for her approach. His brown eyes lit up and he was smiling.

Nope, she decided, thinking that she'd reached her limit for terrible people for the day. As if Georgia showing up hadn't been bad enough.

Kaity drew a deep breath, rallied, and strode past Gabe into the studio, for once not missing Anabelle at her side during a particularly bold endeavor. He opened his mouth as though to say something, and she just kept walking, mentally talking herself up the entire time, and kept up the momentum until she had almost collapsed at the front desk, where Jenny stood in front of a computer.

"Welcome back!" Jenny said cheerily. "Let me get you checked in for class, and then we'll start in a few minutes. We're in the studio to the far right, Studio 1."

Her thoughts still awhirl, Kaity spun around and marched into the studio, clutching her purse and phone. So much for terrible people.

Gabe had prepared what to say to Kaity—something a little flirty, but not too strong a come-on—and then she breezed by him as though he didn't exist. He held the door open as she walked right into Snapdragon, and then let it shut. He could take a hint. Besides, he was full of queso, and he'd just now quickly run some more photos by Jenny that he wanted to use on his website to promote his more artsy endeavors. Mission accomplished. He could get out of Cahrmel and back to M-town proper, which was less hoity-toity and more his speed.

Spending time in Cahrmel always reminded him of his family, anyway. They didn't live there anymore, but the haughty vibe was the same.

The late March sun was shining, warming Gabe's face. Maybe an impromptu outdoors shoot was more his speed today. His thoughts wandered to one of the models he'd worked with last year, and gone on a coffee date/pseudo-date with afterwards. Maybe she'd be available today. Maybe his day would turn around after all.

Kaity found herself in the same studio where the performance had occurred. It was a large rectangle, but when she'd last been there, the outer rim had been filled with folding chairs, a few rows deep, with only two poles in the center visible.

Now she saw that the two poles in the center remained, and there were poles around the edges of the room too. One wall was entirely covered in mirrors, and the wall opposite it had shelves and hooks on the wall. Kaity supposed that she was meant to stash her stuff there, and she saw that there were already a few women congregating around the shelves. Some seemed to already know each other, based on their easy banter, and Kaity found herself missing Anabelle more than ever.

She put her purse on a shelf, and took off her running shoes and socks, since everyone else seemed to already be barefoot. She'd gotten the memo to bring a yoga mat, so she kept it under one arm as she surveyed the scene.

The mirror was obviously at the front of the room, so step one was to pick a pole in the back of the room. The other women milling around seemed to be on the same page, though, so Kaity asserted herself by stepping towards the closest pole in the back row to the door, and dropping her mat in front of it.

Having left her phone in her purse, there was no good way to fidget, so Kaity continued to check out the studio. The back and front rows had three poles each, while the middle row had four, including the two in the center that Kaity remembered from the performance. They were all spaced out from one another, so that if she stood between any two poles, she wouldn't be able to touch them both with her hands extended.

The other two back-row poles were claimed by two women of really different ages, maybe a mother and daughter, who chattered rapidly in Spanish. Directly in front of Kaity was a young woman wearing shorts that showed long, pale legs covered in tattoos. She made eye contact with Kaity, face impassive and darkly-painted lips turned down. Kaity turned away abruptly, hoping she was not in for an hour of being surrounded by judgmental mean girls.

The door to the lobby opened abruptly, and Jenny strode in, wearing joggers and a sweatshirt in a fuchsia that matched the walls of the studio, the same bright vivid magenta as the inside of a snapdragon in bloom.

"Welcome to Pole Basics!" She strode to one of the center two poles and set down a water bottle, a phone, and a notebook. "If you're new to pole, don't worry, we're starting from the ground up. In each class, I'll take us through a warm-up and some stretches, and then we'll learn some moves to string together in a combo, which we'll run to music on the last class." Jenny paused to reach up and redo her blond ponytail. "Please don't hesitate to ask if you have questions; I'm always happy to offer adjustments and modifications because while beginning pole can be tough, it's not supposed to hurt!"

Kaity hoped that it wouldn't be any worse than that indoor cycling class Anabelle had dragged her to last month. Then she mimicked Jenny in unrolling her yoga mat so that it was parallel to the mirrored front wall of the room.

Jenny briefly picked her phone back up, and suddenly the studio was filled with the rambunctious rhythm of one of the songs that was popular right now, though the name escaped Kaity. Jenny led the women through a series of squats, jumping jacks, and lunges, and then talked them through a series of downward-facing dog and tabletop poses. It definitely was not as bad as indoor cycling; Kaity's quads had been so sore she couldn't easily go down stairs for a week afterward.

Kaity found her coordination lacking when they flipped onto their backs to do elongated bicycle-style legs, and soon her abs were burning. She wasn't sure whether to curse or envy Anabelle for missing out on this portion.

After three songs had passed and Jenny deemed them appropriately warmed up, she directed them to put up their yoga mats, grab water as needed, and also grab from the front of the room a small towel and spray bottle of alcohol.

Right then, Anabelle dashed in, still in her work clothes. She apologized to Jenny, who directed her to do a quick warm-up of her own once she was changed, and then join in the class.

"All right, everyone," Jenny said to the rest of them. "The first step is learning how to engage your arm safely while holding on to the pole. The first move we'll learn is the Pole Walk."

Kaity listened attentively. She was good at learning; heck, she learned how to teach and taught how to learn for a living!

After a demonstration of how *not* to do it—as in, not engaging one's shoulders, which left Jenny sagging from the pole like a sad yet adorable kitten hanging from a tablecloth by one claw—Jenny instructed everyone to engage their shoulder blades and pull them down their backs. Then they were supposed to extend their inside arm, the one closest to the pole, upwards while standing to the side of the pole. Everyone faced the mirror, and everyone started with their right arm extended.

Then, they were supposed to take a few tentative steps around the pole, holding it for balance. Two of the other women immediately leaned into their hips, so that each step became swaying and seductive. Kaity counted herself lucky to have not fallen yet.

Anabelle emerged from the bathroom, in a neon pink set of bicycle shorts and matching sports bra. She pounded out some squats and jumping jacks and then walked to the only open pole, one that was directly next to Jenny, waving at Kaity as she walked by.

After the walk—first walking normally, then on the balls of their feet—came the step-around. Kaity listened intently as Jenny described it: weight on the inside foot, inside arm high on the pole, lean out and step around the pole, bringing the outside foot around so as to almost be parallel to the inside foot. It was a big step, and Jenny gracefully demonstrated it, the toe of her stepping foot pointed.

Kaity nervously flashed Anabelle a thumbs-up before trying. Resolved to get the move on her first try, she swung around the pole, got it caught in her armpit, let go in shock, and fell to the ground on her butt. The impact surprised her more than it hurt, but she felt her eyes pricking with new tears, because of course she would mess up while already having a bad day.

"You okay?" Jenny asked. Kaity nodded. Jenny returned to talking the other women through the step, somehow managing to have her attention simultaneously on all parts of the room.

Kaity picked herself up and tried again. It went better this time. Jenny then encouraged everyone to try it on their other side, provoking nervous laughter in the group. Anabelle immediately went for it and did a competent step-around. Now that Kaity knew not to swing so enthusiastically that she got tangled up and fell, she managed a halfway decent step-around on her left side as well.

They all practiced walking around the pole and adding a step-around. Jenny taught them how to switch sides so they could practice on both sides easily. This involved keeping the inside arm high and weight on the inside leg, then lifting the outside knee (toe pointed, of course), and swiveling to face the opposite direction. When the now-inside leg was put down, the now-inside arm joined it. Kaity used this technique to walk around the pole with her right hand on it, and then switch so that her left hand was on it. Switching from left to right involved banging her ankle on the pole more than she liked, but at least she didn't fall again.

After a lesson on how to slide down with one's back on the pole to a seat on the floor, class ended.

Kaity practically pounced on Anabelle as they were gathering their things.

"You will not believe the day I had today!"

True to form, Anabelle perked up around her armful of work clothes, yoga mat, and purse. "Oh, yeah? Want to tell me about it over margaritas? There's a Mexican restaurant a few doors down."

Kaity exited the studio, leaving behind unknown quantities and potential mean girls and the shame of being the first one to fall on her butt in class. She and Anabelle proceeded to get a booth in the Mexican restaurant, order chips and salsa and margaritas, and linger over the dinner options. And there were a lot of options.

"I don't know," Anabelle was saying, "we just did, like, a lot of strength things. That's an argument for fajitas in my book."

"Mm," Kaity replied around a mouthful of chips. "I still think I might get a salad." She suspected that her abject failure in pole class was due to her ample thighs, hips, and butt.

They compromised and split an order of fajitas. Then they toasted to a girls' night out.

"Today was terrible," Kaity announced. And then amended, "Er, mostly. Pole class with you was fun."

"What was terrible?" Anabelle asked.

Kaity put her glass down to bury her head in her hands. "My ex-sister-in-law showed up at my workplace...because I helped her get a job there." Anabelle screwed up her cute little nose in disgust. "Yeah, I know, it's my fault. But she was so *nice* at first."

Anabelle said, "Remind me why we hate her?" In that moment, Kaity remembered why Anabelle was one of her best friends. Regardless, Kaity fidgeted with the salt rim on her glass for a heartbeat before answering.

"Okay, we'd just moved here. Me and John. It was for his work more than mine, and because he has family here. I'd met them before, but I was trying to make a good impression, like, we were recently married, and I wanted them to know I'd take care of him." Kaity paused when their food arrived, and then she and Anabelle were busy dividing up their fajitas.

"I offered to get his sister a job, which is obviously how she ended up at my company. But I wasn't thinking about it long-term...I wasn't happy here. I don't have friends here..." she paused, and amended, "well, I didn't 'til now." Anabelle beamed in response.

"I was hanging out with Georgia one night to work on her resume. And we split a bottle of wine, and she asked, and I opened up about how I wasn't thrilled with our move from Louisville to Mariontown." Kaity sighed, remembering the conversation and its aftermath. "Next thing I knew, she'd tattled on me to John, and he was asking if I wanted to get a divorce. I didn't have time to suggest couples therapy or anything."

Anabelle was silent for a moment. "You haven't told me this story before." Her chipper tone bordered on accusatory to Kaity's ears.

Kaity squirmed a bit. "I know. I don't like to talk about it. I don't want there to be a villain in my story, I don't want to hate Georgia or John or anyone. I don't want to be the poor victimized divorced woman."

Anabelle reached out to cover Kaity's hand with her own.

"You have the right to feel how you feel. And based on what you've said in the past, it sounds like John didn't actually listen to you, wasn't there for you when you guys moved here, and wasn't with you for the right reasons. It's okay to tell your story how you experienced it."

Kaity freed her hand to grab another chip, dunk it in salsa, and eat it, so she could pretend that the tears forming in the corners of her eyes were from the spiciness.

"I...thanks, Anabelle. You're a true friend."

Lips turned up devilishly, Anabelle said, "Duh. So, what are we wearing to pole class next week?"

Chapter 6

B y week two of pole class, Anabelle knew everyone else's names: Andrea and Maricela, an aunt and niece who decided to take the class together; Miriam, the goth-looking young woman who'd given Kaity the cold shoulder on the first day of class; and then Lin, Laila, Alyssa, and Jasmine, who were all friends in their 20s and liked to sample different fitness classes around town.

Kaity managed a smile in everyone's direction but that was about it.

She'd managed to avoid Georgia at work easily enough, because training modules ate most of the new-comer's time, and with the spring semester ending soon, Kaity's plate was full of module prep for the various universities around town. Summer was a great time to catch up new hires on Title IX regulations, technology security trainings, and the like, so Kaity got to construct trainings, checking each one against the institution's values, goals, and budget.

The second week of pole class also involved learning a fireman's spin, which left Kaity's ankles bruised to all hell. She and Anabelle had opted for a Broad River restaurant for dinner that evening, Top Cat, and they were digging into burgers and sweet potato fries when Anabelle lifted her eyes to the restaurant's door.

"Hey, isn't that the cute photographer?"

Kaity dreaded the thought, but she looked anyway. Yes, it was Gabe. She put down her half-eaten burger to dab at her mouth—and cheeks, and chin—with her napkin just in case. The two women visually tracked him to the bar, where he sat and ordered a drink. Maybe he was meeting with a client, and couldn't talk.

She turned to Anabelle to say something along those lines, and caught Anabelle waving at Gabe, gesturing for him to come join them.

"What are you doing?!" Kaity hissed.

"He's cute, and I don't think you gave him a fair shot," Anabelle replied.

"Well then, *you* go out with him!" Kaity shot back.

Anabelle's face clouded. "I'm not ready to date yet."

"That's my line," Kaity complained.

By then, Gabe had reached their table, a pint in his hand.

"Hi," he said, and smiled bashfully. "We saw each other at the Snapdragon showcase, right? Can you remind me of your names?"

Inwardly groaning to herself that he didn't remember running into her a week ago, Kaity introduced herself, and then Anabelle introduced herself. Within minutes, Anabelle and Gabe had established having a friend in common.

Kaity sat silently, feeling reminded of how much she didn't belong here.

Gabe then turned towards her, unleashing a brilliant smile. "We've got a joke here in Mariontown: there are only two social groups, the people you know and the people they know." As much as she didn't want to like him or his smile, Kaity found herself returning a friendly expression.

"So, you just moved here, right?" Gabe asked her, while Anabelle surreptitiously excused herself to go use the bathroom.

"Yes, in the middle of last year," Kaity replied. She didn't like talking about the divorce, but she found herself explaining that she'd moved here with her husband, and then found herself without one.

Gabe made a sympathetic noise. "Sorry to hear that."

"It's for the best," Kaity explained. "It turns out that we weren't a good fit after all, and I had some issues with his family." She didn't know how to read his expressions yet, but it looked like something both intense and sad was happening on Gabe's face. It was gone in the next moment.

"Hey, do you model?" he asked. Kaity started in her seat.

"Um, for what?"

"Photoshoots. I'm thinking about doing a new series, since I've met a lot of dancers through Snapdragon, like a collection of mini-narratives chronicling everyone's journey, paired with classical art periods."

Kaity understood most of those words. She worked with graphic designers regularly, who often had loftier artistic ambitions. But she got stuck on the implication that she could be a model.

"I...uh..."

She also got stuck on the idea of Gabe looking at her for extended periods of time.

"You don't mean nude modeling, right?" she asked, and then felt alternately embarrassed for even thinking it, and proud for sticking up for herself in case that turned out to be the case, and indignant that he might think she'd just whip off her clothing for him.

Gabe just chuckled. "No, that's a whole separate discussion. This would definitely be a clothed shoot."

Anabelle chose that time to return. Gabe passed a business card to Kaity, saying, "I'll let you two get back to your dinner. Here's how to reach me if you're interested."

After cursory farewells, Anabelle turned to Kaity. "Did he just ask you out? Tell me he just asked you out!"

"I don't think so?" Kaity turned the business card over in her hands. The front was an image of a couple in bridal attire standing beneath a gorgeous flowered trellis, no doubt to advertise that he did wedding shoots, and did them well. On the other side of the card, a human back, muscles thrown into relief by stark lighting, faded into the words with Gabe's full name, website, email, and phone number.

"I think he wants me to model for a photoshoot? But I don't get why he didn't ask you too," Kaity said. "He made it sound like he was gonna ask everyone at Snapdragon because it's a new concept of women being photographed in a series of stories."

"You do have a story to tell," Anabelle reminded Kaity. "Remember? You were unhappy in your marriage and now you're free! Anyway, I think he's interested in you but not in me, which is fine...I'd get bored sitting in one pose for so long!"

Kaity turned the business card over in her hands a few more times, her gaze lingering on the nude back: neck, shoulders, spine.

"We'll see," she said.

Gabe went back to the bar, sipping his local draft, and thought about how he'd feature Kaity in pre-Raphaelite garb to tell whatever story of her life she wanted to tell. His invitation had been a bit spontaneous; granted, he was working with various dancers from Snapdragon on putting together some shoots, but nothing had really come together cohesively yet. The showcase was over, but many of the dancers were preparing for a pole convention in St. Louis. A narrative angle would be nice, though. It'd give everyone a lot of leeway to interpret things how they wanted to.

His previous two attempts to go on dates in the last week had both fizzled. The woman he'd been talking to on Tinder had called him flighty, of all things, as though he wasn't extremely dedicated to his career. So dedicated, in fact, that not only was he booked most weekends at weddings, but he spent most days and nights either editing photos or chasing down new work, only sometimes getting to collaborate on the more creative stuff that actually gave him joy.

His family might not recognize it, but he had a re-spectable career. One he worked for. As if that would erase the past.

After glowering at his empty pint glass, Gabe sat for a moment, alone in the hubbub. He was on the fence about ordering a second pint when he saw Kaity and Anabelle get up to leave. The sudden urge to go walk up to Kaity seized him, and he fought it. He had to let her come to him; he couldn't be perceived as too aggressive in chasing down models.

Which, he reflected, gave him a good idea for a shoot. It might not be *her* story, but it was a story she'd be good in.

Gabe settled up and left the brewpub, itching to get his hands on some of his old art school books. Oh, this was going to be fun.

Kaity and Anabelle lingered in front of their cars before going to their respective apartments.

"I think you should do it," Anabelle was saying. "It's the perfect reclaim-your-life move! And maybe reclaim your sexuality too!" she winked.

Kaity rolled her eyes. "I haven't had sex in almost a year. My ex made a point of telling me I was too fat to be attractive well before we got divorced."

"Hey, look at me," Anabelle said. Kaity found herself staring slightly down into Anabelle's green eyes. "You have curves. That's normal. You could be bigger, you could be smaller, but you'd still be *you*. Your piece of shit ex didn't deserve you. Mine pulled similar crap with me, and it took a while to get over. So I'm saving you lots of money on therapy by insisting that you learn to feel sexy again on your own terms."

Kaity felt a small pinch in her chest, like she was going to cry. Then the intensity vanished from Anabelle's gaze and she put on her normal smile. "Seriously. It could be fun. It could be a different side of you. Regardless of whether you hook up with him, it's worth a shot."

Unable to resist rolling her eyes again, Kaity snorted. "Hook up? What, is this college?" But she had to admit, maybe Anabelle was right about learning to be sexy again. She hadn't really entertained the thought that she would immediately become a sex goddess by taking a few weeks' worth of pole dance classes, but it did feel good to nail the step-around without losing her grip and falling. It felt good to leave class with her arms sore (and her abs, and her legs, because of that new move that involved hooking a knee around the pole and running one's hands down one's standing leg and flipping one's hair on the way up, all the while attempting to not look like a drunk flamingo).

"Selfie time!" Anabelle declared, and whipped her phone out. Kaity realized she had no idea where her phone was, and patted her pockets until she found it. She smiled at Anabelle's phone, so they could document their evening and send it to the rest of the group chat as evidence that divorced ladyfriends could in fact be out on a Monday night living it up.

Kaity eased her phone back into her pocket. Her hands were a little sore from pole, so she didn't need to be clutching the darn thing 24/7, she told herself. But really, she was waiting to get on her phone so she could decide whether to email or text Gabe, and what to tell him. Part of her thought, it's been six months since your divorce, so maybe it's time to explore. Even if it just ends up being friendly. And maybe it'd help her work up the courage to do something else in that vein, like do a boudoir photoshoot or actually try online dating.

She and Anabelle said good night to one another after making plans for Kaity to swing by the following evening and help Anabelle with some work stuff. On the short drive back to her apartment, Kaity reflected on how maybe this new chapter in her life didn't suck after all.

Chapter 7

After another week of keeping her head down at work and trying to avoid Georgia, Kaity arrived early at Snapdragon for her class. She deliberately put her phone down instead of checking her work emails, though there was one subject line that hinted at a social function for new employees (with old employees of course encouraged to attend). That just sounded painful.

Jenny said she could go into Studio 1 as there wasn't a class beforehand, so she went in to claim her pole and practice her step-around and fireman's spin. Within a few minutes, someone joined her: Miriam. Kaity wasn't sure if she was in the right headspace for a conversation, so she just smiled and kept practicing.

"Hey," Miriam said.

Kaity stopped without banging into anything, and returned the greeting.

"You look like you remember the sequence from last week. Could you walk me through it?"

Shocked, Kaity said sure, and walked over her purse to grab her little notebook. She gazed back at Miriam to find the tall girl's dark eyes on her. Today's lipstick was peacock blue, and her long dark hair was swept high in a ponytail. She's the one who should be modeling, Kaity found herself thinking, and she tried to think it without too much acrimony.

Kaity ran through the combination of moves they'd just put together, and Miriam replicated them on her own pole. She moved with a grace that Kaity envied, though a new idea occurred to Kaity as she watched Miriam bang her ankles and her knees during the fireman's spin: maybe being tall and slender could be a liability in pole. More real estate to bang up. The few times Kaity had fallen on her butt, she'd had plenty of padding to absorb it, whereas when Miriam took a small tumble, as she did just now, it looked like it actually hurt.

They walked through the combo twice before everyone else arrived and class began.

"Thank you," Miriam said. As Kaity replied "You're welcome," she noticed that Miriam's face looked just as serious no matter what she was saying or doing. Feeling chagrined, she wondered if she'd misjudged her on day one of class.

Jenny showed them new and torturous things, and instructed everyone to come wearing shorts next week so they could begin to learn a basic climb. Half of the women were already wearing shorts, but Kaity exchanged a panicked look with Maricela, who was on the pole next to her, and was also probably of an age to recall when extra thigh fat was called saddlebags.

They packed up their things so the next class could enter, and Kaity stuck close to Anabelle as usual, but this time with a different purpose.

"Can we ask Miriam to join us for dinner?"

"Ooh yes, good idea!" Anabelle replied. She forged ahead to catch Miriam as she put on knee-length black boots with zippers and other metallic things dangling off them.

"Hey, Miriam, want to grab a bite with us? We usually get dinner after pole class each week," Anabelle said with a grin.

"I can't, I have to study tonight," Miriam said, zipping up her boots. She paused. "But next week should work, so, thanks for thinking of me. Also, I'm mostly vegetarian, if that's okay?"

"Totally fine!" Anabelle beamed. "Between here and Broad River there are a half dozen spots that would work."

Kaity nodded and felt compelled to chime in. "Four Sisters near me in SoBro is good."

"Cool," Miriam said, and then headed out.

Once Kaity and Anabelle were ensconced in a booth at a Japanese restaurant between Cahrmel and Broad River, Anabelle ordered Kaity to update her on the photoshoot.

"There's nothing to update," Kaity said. "I actually emailed Gabe on Friday afternoon and haven't heard back."

"Weird," Anabelle said. "He seemed into you, or at least into the idea of doing something artsy with you."

Kaity shrugged, and pointed to the sushi rolls she wanted to order. Anabelle concurred on each choice, and suggested adding edamame as an appetizer. Then they ordered iced green tea as well.

"I enjoyed the idea of being someone else, someone sexier, even if it was just a brief fantasy. Maybe I missed being wanted, since it's been a while. But it's okay." Kaity's smile felt brittle. She wasn't sure if it *was* okay, but she intended to put on a brave front for Anabelle. Anabelle bought it, anyway, and their conversation turned to work complaints.

Once she got home, pleasantly full of sushi, Kaity checked her email on her phone and saw a reply from Gabe. He apologized, saying he'd been working all weekend, but he was still interested in the shoot, and maybe she could come to his studio on Thursday evening to discuss possibilities.

He ended with a question: did she know anything about Greek mythology?

Kaity found herself intrigued. She made herbal tea, curled up on the loveseat in her living room, and got out one of the few books from college that she hadn't lost in the divorce. It was world mythology, and she remembered where the Greek mythology section was. What could Gabe possibly have in mind?

Gabe was relieved when Kaity wrote back that same evening that she was available, and would he please send her the address of his studio.

He hadn't meant to drop the ball with this one, really. Especially not after being called flighty.

But he had in fact worked all weekend with back-to-back weddings, and then his stepmother had actually tried to come to his apartment, small crummy thing that it was, to demand to talk to him and work things out. Like she always did when he stopped answering her texts. As though it would change anything.

Neither of them could go back and change the past. Their family was broken, and Gabe didn't have the inclination to try to fix it, not when his stepmother was intent on manipulating the truth.

Well, he had one reason to try to fix things. But his stepmother was too big an obstacle, as always.

Gabe texted Kaity his studio address, then tossed his phone down. He had his own life to live now. And if he could make this project with Kaity everything he'd envisioned, with other models to follow, sharing art and stories and more, maybe he'd find some healing of his own, too.

His phone buzzed. Surely Kaity hadn't already responded?

No. It was his stepmother.

Except...it was an invitation. For Easter dinner. With the dangle of a lure that Gabe had half been expecting: if he showed up to family meal and acted civilized, his mom would *consider* letting him reconnect with his sister.

Even if it was just a chance, it was better than nothing. But how was he going to convince his conservative stepmother that he'd cleaned up his act and was responsible? She hated his artistic side, always had, so his moderate paycheck from wedding photography wouldn't mean anything to her.

There had to be a way.

Chapter 8

Thursday morning found Kaity at her desk, pre-pared for a long day of compiling trainings with her usual mug of tea. But the work grew tedious, and even Kaity's normally meticulous attention to detail began to give out.

Caffeine, she thought longingly, then stopped short.

Georgia had become the social butterfly of the office and spent a lot of her time in the break room/kitchen, which meant that Kaity had chosen to seclude herself in her office more often than not. Being faced with a gloating reminder of her failed marriage was not her idea of a good time. Obviously she couldn't hide forever, but until she figured out how to deal with Georgia and her complicated feelings around the whole thing, this was the best option.

Her eyes blurred on the computer screen, forcing her decision, and also encouraging her to put a note into her calendar on her phone to either get a hot water kettle for her office or to pack two travel mugs of tea next time.

Hoping for an empty break room, Kaity slunk in, and rummaged in the free fridge until she found a bottle of cold brew coffee. Not her favorite, but she appreciated a company that looked after the caffeine levels of its employees. Next, she found cream. She turned away from the fridge, hoping to make it out unscathed, when she saw Georgia lounging in the doorway.

"Midmorning break already?" Georgia asked.

Kaity nodded, unsure whether to dignify the question with a response. "I'm just heading back to my office now."

"Well, don't let me stop you," Georgia said, stepping into the room and leaving the doorway empty.

Kaity made a break for it, then froze when she heard Georgia's voice behind her.

"I was just wondering, though...with the company party in a month, will you have a plus-one?" Kaity spun around, looking for a mocking glint in Georgia's eyes but finding a veneer of innocence.

"What—?" Kaity sputtered.

"Oh, I just meant, are you *allowed* to bring a plus-one? A guest, or perhaps a partner, or a spouse if you were still married. I'm still new here," and with that, Georgia let the venom creep into her smile.

Calming her breathing with effort, Kaity replied, "I'm sure it says on the invite as it always does. One guest per employee. And yes, I'm bringing someone." Then she spun around and strode back to her office before Georgia could fire off another shot.

Trying to focus on job instead of how much she hated Georgia—and by extension, her ex-husband John—turned out to be too much work. Kaity finished her cold brew and put her head into her hands, resting on her desk. Why had she said she was bringing someone? She could always bring Anabelle, but what if

Anabelle were busy on that date? And would Kaity risk looking like she wasn't over her ex yet if she showed up with a friend? Georgia would probably be reporting back to John about whatever happened at the work party, unless he'd grown up and moved on with his life in the interim. Flashing back to when John had jealously read some of the text messages on her phone back when they lived in Louisville, Kaity deemed that unlikely.

This couldn't go on, Kaity decided. But it wasn't like she could complain to Antonio about Georgia; she didn't have any evidence that Georgia had wronged her, and pretty much everything that came out of Georgia's mouth could be interpreted in alternatively more or less sinister ways, so accusing her of verbal abuse or harassment was right out. Maybe if she showed up Georgia at the company party, Georgia would move on and focus on her own life rather than trying to take Kaity down to her level.

The idea that occurred to Kaity was wild enough that, by all rights, it should have emerged from its cocoon in Anabelle's head, not hers. At this point, though, she would try anything, even if it risked humiliation at the hands of a cute photographer.

Towards six, Kaity pulled up at the address Gabe had given her. She hadn't explored this part of M-town yet, though she'd heard from other divorced ladyfriends that Fountain Circle had cute shops and restaurants. The big brick building he'd described—the McMurphy Building—was easy to locate. His studio, nestled within the labyrinth inside, was not.

As usual, Kaity had left herself a bit of "getting lost/minor panic attack/anxiety attack" time, so she arrived in front of his door right around 6:15 as he'd suggested.

She knocked, and there was Gabe, smiling and ushering her in. Kaity had to admit to herself that he looked really cute when he smiled.

The studio was a narrow, rectangular space, with one of the long walls covered in a large cream-colored piece of cloth. Natural light, fading though it was, entered from a window on one of the narrow walls. Prints of photos in all sizes were hung on the remaining walls and scattered on shelving. Gabe led her to a little sitting area, with three armchairs, all covered in different fabrics, pulled together around a small metal lattice table.

He gestured for her to sit, and smiled at her hesitation in picking a seat. "I usually have a bride and groom coming in together, or the bride with her bestie, hence there being three seats."

"I see," Kaity said, remembering for a few moments her own wedding, a little over five years ago. It had been a joyous occasion, not a cloud in the sky, as though nature itself declined to say whether or not her marriage would turn out well.

She ended up picking an armchair with a bright orange and green paisley print. As Kaity made herself comfortable and put her purse down on the floor, Gabe started describing the new photo series he had in mind. It was just a side project, he made sure to say, as though reassuring her that nothing would be taken too seriously in case it didn't work out. But he'd already spoken to some of the other women at Snapdragon about the possibility of doing a themed shoot, and they'd expressed interest.

Taking the first step in hopefully being brave, Kaity asked, "So where do I come in?"

Gabe smiled another beautiful smile, ran a hand through his brown curls and said, "You'll be my first! The first model I shoot, I mean. I actually prefer working with people who don't have a lot of modeling experience for these more experimental projects, since they have fewer preconceived notions. We'll brainstorm together which Greek myth tells your story, and then we'll shoot it. I've got a standard waiver, of course, but that's for later."

"I started looking up myths using an old college book, but honestly, I'm not sure which one fits me," Kaity replied. She made a mental note to have a legal friend read the waiver over before signing it.

"That's the beauty of it," Gabe said. "We can figure it out, get you placed in an artistic time period too, and then shoot. There's no rush. It's about the process."

"Um, okay." Kaity suspected she wasn't very good at "the process," especially if it meant trusting people and being present in the moment. She steadied herself by imagining meeting her future goals, like dealing with Georgia and working up the courage to wear pole shorts.

"This isn't related, but can I ask you something?"

"Sure," Gabe answered. He stood to retrieve a couple of books from a nearby shelf.

"I've got this work function in a month, and, it's complicated, but I need to bring a date. Would you be open to something like that? Just be my arm candy?"

Gabe had sat back down and was leafing through one of the books. A page fell open, showing the three graces in flowing robes.

Kaity liked his eyes, but she did not like how he was staring at her. She realized that she should have prepared an apology in case things went sideways. As they clearly had. She had misjudged his intentions, the whole "let's talk about art" thing, assuming that would mean, like, spending time together, getting to know each other, possible friendship on the table, all the sorts of exchanges that might lead to, say, floating a kinda wacky idea and having it go over well. Oh god, he was still staring.

"That's it," he said slowly.

"What's what?" Kaity asked weakly, wondering if she had messed this up beyond all recognition.

"I think you just helped me solve one of my problems too. If I come be your date, will you come be mine?"

Kaity blinked. She had not been expecting a reciprocal arrangement.

"To...what? And when?"

Gabe shut the book in front of him and leaned back in his chair, staring at the ceiling.

"I have...problems... with my family. My younger sister is still a minor, and our mom, technically my stepmother, won't let me talk to her most of the time. She doesn't even have a cell phone. And unless I show up to family functions full of obnoxiously repentant behavior, another half year goes by before we can have any meaningful contact."

"I'm sorry, that's awful" Kaity said. Gabe shifted his attention to her, and Kaity felt the weight of those warm brown eyes.

"I don't usually talk about it," Gabe said, "but thank you."

"My stuff is...well, it's related to my divorce. It'd help me with a problem to have someone with me." That was all Kaity could get out.

"So, a fake date this month for Easter, and one next month for your work thing?" Gabe asked.

Kaity nodded. "We're already hanging out for this photo series, so we could learn enough about each other to make it convincing."

Gabe smiled devilishly. "Good point. But if we're doing this, we're doing it right. I've gotta take you to my favorite first date spot. Have you had dinner yet?"

As Gabe grabbed a book to bring for research purposes and texted Kaity the name of the restaurant, he felt a lightness in his movements that hadn't been there for a while. Yes, spring wedding season was a grind, and yes, his stepmother was generally awful... but he couldn't believe he hadn't thought of this before. Kaity seemed so nice, and she was cute and intelligent enough to impress his family and be a plausible partner for him, given his artistic eye.

He also paused to lift a light jacket from the coat rack near the door; it was vain, but he knew the blazer looked good on him. Oh, and his phone was plugged into the charger still, so he pocketed both phone and charger, knowing that he'd probably space out and let his battery die if he didn't.

Even if his family continued to judge him for not having a respectable career, they could acknowledge that he'd brought home a beautiful woman who adored him. Gabe hoped that if she expected him to return the favor, she'd be ready to play the part.

And as long as it was just play, everyone would get what they wanted.

Chapter 9

K aity drove around Fountain Circle with its maddening diagonal intersections, found the restaurant Gabe had directed her to, and went to stand inside, as there was still a bit of early spring chill in the air.

The Silver Ring was bigger than a hole-in-the-wall restaurant, but not by much. Kaity's initial loud impression of gaudy red walls was soothed by dark wooden furniture. A burnished wooden bar took up much of the room, with a mix of low- and high-top tables throughout the remainder of the main room.

Gabe tapped Kaity on the shoulder, having entered a few minutes behind her, and she whirled around to face him.

"Do you have a preference for where we sit?" he asked. She shook her head.

He caught a server's eye, and then led Kaity to a low-ish table that was somewhat secluded, as it was on the far wall from the bar. He pulled out Kaity's chair for her, earning him first-date points in her mind...if they had been on an actual date.

The server came over with menus; she was waif-thin and heavily pierced.

"How's it going, Gabe?" she asked. As he responded, Kaity reminded herself that this was not a real date, so it didn't matter if he was on first-name terms with the server at the restaurant where he'd just said he normally brought first dates.

Kaity turned her attention to the menu. If this wasn't actually a date, then the rules of what to eat or not eat on a first date likely didn't apply. Then again, she'd spent much of the last year getting divorced, and had been married for five years prior, plus engaged/seriously dating two years before then, so it was probably that she was out of the loop on dating dos-and-don'ts anyway.

Try not to overthink it, she reminded herself. So she asked: "What's good here?"

Gabe had barely glanced at the menu. "I usually get the southwest chicken wrap or meatball sliders. They have a few local beers on tap, a nice cocktail list, and a handful of wines, too."

Kaity opted for a taco salad, and a glass of chardonnay. She worried that white wine was too stereotypical, and reminded herself not to worry; this was just an arrangement.

The metallic-studded server, whose name was Tanya, came back to take their orders and also the menus. Once that was done, Gabe leaned back in his chair, regarding Kaity speculatively.

"So, we move our meeting date back a few weeks to just over a month, and we had our first date shortly after, then it would make sense that I invite you to Easter with my family."

She pulled a notebook out of her purse. "Yes, I could've run into you at Snapdragon or had Anabelle's mutual friend introduce us, hmm, around the middle of February. I would've been free then, since my company generally has more down time between the start of the spring semester and spring break."

Gabe's eyebrows had risen when she looked up from her notebook.

"You...have a notebook? You're writing this down?"

Kaity bit her lower lip. "...yes? It's what I do?"

Gabe chuckled, and Kaity relaxed a hair. "I have to stay decently organized for my work, but this is taking it to a whole new level." She must've visibly flinched, because he continued on to say, "Not that it's a problem. We *should* have a unified story to tell my family and your coworkers."

She smiled hesitantly. Not being judged for her meticulous, anxious habits was a new feeling. Her ex had accused her of never leaving work at work, but he had also relied on her to make sure the household bills were all paid on time, so she was never quite sure how defensive to be about her particular skill set.

"Okay, cool," Kaity replied. Her wine was set down right then, so she took a sip, gathering her thoughts.

"So, we met a little over a month ago, had our first date here...and while dating, you proposed this photo series idea?"

Gabe nodded. One of his brown curls fell into his face, and he brushed his hair out of his eyes with one hand before leaning back in his seat, drink in his other hand.

"And when I introduce my family, you...what do you do, again?"

"I'm an instructional designer," Kaity replied. "I work downtown. Mostly I make modules for all the local colleges, so they can keep all their trainings up to date. I like it, and it pays the bills."

"And you're not, like, actually with anyone else right now?" Gabe asked.

"Oh. Very much no. Recently divorced and all."

The words hung between them, heavy in the cramped space of the restaurant.

"Okay," Gabe said. "Wait, how old are you?"

"I'm thirty-four," Kaity said. "How old are *you?*"

"Thirty," he said.

Kaity had another sip of wine while pondering this new development. "Your family won't think I'm a cougar, will they? Is four years considered a big age difference at this point?"

Gabe shrugged. "I haven't had a serious girlfriend in years, so I have no idea."

"Okay, so maybe we don't mention the age difference or the divorce," Kaity suggested. The whole point was to keep things simple, right?

Gabe paused. "If you don't mind me asking, what happened? Like in your marriage. You seem like a great person so far."

Kaity froze. Set her wine glass down. Folded her hands in.

"I don't think I'm ready to talk about it," she whispered.

Gabe leaned across the table and hesitated just before patting her on the shoulder. He withdrew. "I'm sorry," he said. "I don't mean to pry, but...I don't want to remind you of anything bad? We're supposed to be playing make believe, this is supposed to be fun and a useful way to cross things off the annoying lists life makes us keep."

Kaity managed a wan smile. "You're fine. I don't think you're much like my ex-husband at all." That much was true; John had suppressed his artistic side to get through a series of web development and software engineering degrees, and then his almost-midlife crisis had hit with a vengeance, leading him to be dissatisfied with everything Kaity did and everything she was. He'd offloaded significant household tasks onto her during the completion of his final degree, despite the fact that they were both working full-time, and then he'd complained about Kaity running the house without giving him a say in the matter.

Her marriage had ended in a baffling series of contradictions. Since divorce, her life had become simpler in so many ways. And, Kaity hoped, this ruse would be just one more simplifying agent.

Gabe had opted for the Korean BBQ sliders rather than his usual picks. This was not, after all, a real date, and it didn't matter how messy he got.

After he'd downed another mouthful of beef, washed down with a local porter, he asked, "I'll probably need to know, are you from around here, or not?"

He watched Kaity put down her fork and dab her mouth with a napkin. She really was beautiful, even if she didn't carry herself like she knew it.

"I grew up in Louisville, went away for college, then came back to work. That's where I met my ex. We got married there, then moved here, since he has family here, and then got divorced." She pronounced the words with a finality that made Gabe a bit sad, as though she expected to forever be alone after that.

He polished off his sliders while she talked, and then used his napkin in a minimalist attempt to clean up.

"Okay, so: you're from Louisville, college, Louisville, married, moved here, work as an instructional designer, divorced...but you have hobbies and other interests, right?" Gabe couldn't imagine a time when he hadn't had photography and art in his life.

Kaity fidgeted. He watched, starting to pick up on her nervous habits. He idly wondered which of them might translate well into a photography, a frozen image of one meaningful moment.

"Anabelle brings me to things. She convinced me to come out to the Snapdragon showcase, where you and I met for the first time. She's the reason I'm taking a pole class right now, even though I'm awful at it. We have other friends in our group for divorced women, and I hang out with them sometimes. Mostly I guess I'm just a homebody. I like to read."

Gabe took a second to make sure his hands were clean before he reached across the table to gently touch her hand. "Hey, it's okay. You don't have to impress me. We're here to help each other out, remember?" His efforts rewarded him with a timid smile.

"Okay, so me. I'm born and raised Mariontown, did a stint on the road after my mom and brother died, art school on the East Coast, settled back here as an adult." He paused, not wanting to dig too deep into those memories. "My dad remarried, tried to get the band back together, but his new wife, my step-mom, who makes me call her Mom, thinks I'm a bad influence on their kid. My half-sister Holly. So I have to do this song and dance with them all the fucking time, just to have a seat at the table." He exhaled. That was a bit more than he'd intended to reveal.

When he looked at Kaity, she appeared sympathetic. Maybe, despite his stepmother's stunning exterior, not everything that came in a pretty package was poison.

And anyway, he might as well have some fun while in this arrangement.

Gabe smiled what he knew was his best winning smile, leaned in, and asked, "Now that we've been dating for over a month, what do we like to do together?"

He watched Kaity's brain doing gymnastics in her head. He thanked his lucky stars that he wasn't actually dating her, since he was a free spirit and she was way too analytical. And, he didn't like admitting this to himself, it was almost like she was signing up for most of the work in making the game of pretend happen. What was wrong with enjoying that?

Kaity got through the meal, and helped brainstorm some of their other date nights: movies, gallery openings, and the like. She thanked Gabe for introducing her to this eccentric little Fountain Circle joint, and then let him walk her to her car.

When they got there, he towered over her, and backed her up, almost so that she was up against her driver's side exterior.

"Is this in the plan?" Kaity whispered. She hadn't been this close to a man in months, not counting her optometrist.

Gabe smiled, and leaned in to kiss her cheek. Then he pulled away, and Kaity found herself missing the warmth of his body.

"We should at least be comfortable with cheek kisses and hand holding. Since we didn't get to talk much about ideas for the photoshoot, we can meet up again next week, get in a bit of boyfriend/girlfriend practice at the same time. And then Easter is coming up."

Kaity nodded, then slid down a bit from under his arms to wedge herself into her car. "Sounds good. Thanks for dinner, bye!" She disliked sounding so perfunctory, but sometimes when she needed to get out of a situation, that's how it was.

She started her car, turned on navigation—for some reason, of all the M-town neighborhoods, getting in and out of Fountain Circle still baffled her—and saw the text message from Anabelle.

Come to think of it, she'd mentioned to Anabelle that she had a devious plan.

Tell. Me. Everything.!!,1!

Chapter 10

The next day was Friday, and while Anabelle tried to convince Kaity to come to a chair-dancing workshop at Snapdragon, Kaity refused to be drawn in further: she had plenty on her plate as it was, with starting to work odd hours and managing the shift from spring semester projects to summer projects.

They compromised and went out for lunch. Since Kaity had more leeway with her day's schedule than Anabelle did, Kaity met Anabelle at a spot near her workplace on the near east side. Irlington was a cute enough neighborhood, full of historic houses and storefronts, and Kaity found the pizza joint, Sockamo's, easily enough.

When Anabelle arrived, she barely glanced at a menu before turning her intense gaze onto Kaity.

"Start from the beginning!" she ordered, leaning forward on her elbows ominously.

"Okay, so, my ex sister-in-law is being a bitch, but you knew that," Kaity said. "I had this wild idea to ask Gabe to be my date at the work party next month, and he actually said yes! Turns out he has some family stuff on his plate, so in return, I'm going to his family's Easter dinner soon."

Anabelle relaxed her stance a little, tilting her head as she pondered.

"Hmmm...so... an exchange is being made, you each get something out of it." She cocked her head. "But tell me again, why do you need someone to come to your work party?"

"Either he can run interference with Georgia so she'll stop picking on me, or she'll run home to her brother to report on how I've already moved on."

"But why is that your goal?" Anabelle asked.

Kaity was reaching for the water, and paused. It really wasn't obvious to Anabelle, was it? Clearly whatever had gone down in her divorce was very different than what had happened in Kaity's.

"John and I went through mediation, not like as an alternative to couples therapy, but as a path to an amicable divorce. This woman was an attorney, and the way John talked to me in front of her, as though she wasn't even there...he yelled at me and called me broken. He said I'd die alone, because I'm too anxious and worthless to ever interest anyone again."

She stopped abruptly, feeling her breath hitch like it had in that moment. Why had he said those things? To guilt her into breaking off the divorce and returning to him, so he could treat her however badly he wanted, since she was convinced that there were no better options for her? Just to vent and use her to absorb all his negative feelings about the matter? Like he'd been doing already in milder ways? Either way, it wasn't right. People in love—or who had been in love—shouldn't talk to each other like that.

"I'm sorry," Anabelle whispered. "That's just not right," as though echoing what had been running through Kaity's mind. "I guess I can see where showing him, by proxy of his sister, that you've moved on...it's a power move. It makes sense, in a way."

The server swung by, and Kaity and Anabelle scrambled to pick up their menus and start their order. Once their order of a salad and pizza to share was in, Anabelle returned her attention to Kaity.

"Okay, so you asked Gabe to be your guest, and then ...?"

Kaity felt a smile reach her face. "We went on a first date. Like, a fake first date. But it would help establish the timeline, give us some shared memories." She reached for her purse, in order to get out her notebook.

Anabelle inhaled sharply, looking aghast. "No, Kaity, *you didn't!*"

"Didn't what?"

"Bring a notebook on a date!"

Kaity rolled her eyes. "That's what he said too! But it wasn't a date, so why does it matter?"

"We are going to have a talk before you go on a for-real date," Anabelle said sternly.

Dismissing that as an empty threat, Kaity opened the notebook and described the rest of the "date" and how it had ended with a kiss on her cheek.

"It was fun, but it wasn't real, and honestly that's fine. I get the sense that he's gone on a lot of first dates there, and whatever, I'm not judging, but I don't think Gabe is the type of commit. Not that I'm looking for commitment right now, having just gotten divorced. But, um, if I were..." she trailed off. No sense revisiting that line of thought too soon. If even the idea of a fake date made her mildly nervous, clearly she wasn't ready for the real thing.

"It does sound like a nice time," Anabelle said be-grudgingly. "I'm just upset you didn't tell me about your plans beforehand. I could've helped you come up with such a nice outfit!"

"But it was a *fake* date," Kaity emphasized. "Once I go on a real date, you can help me get ready!" An-abelle's fashion sense was somewhat different than hers, Anabelle being five-ish years younger than Kaity, but getting dressed with a friend might be fun and festive.

That promise seemed to perk Anabelle up, and then the arrival of food perked them both up, and for a time Kaity forgot all of the unpleasant reasons why she'd needed a fake date in the first place. The creole pizza they shared was tasty, and unlike anything Kaity could get in Louisville despite it being further south than Mar-iontown. She still had to decide: would she stick to her plan to leave town in less than three months, if things didn't work out here? And how would she tell Anabelle?

Chapter 11

W edging herself into a set of bicycle shorts was not Kaity's idea of a good time, but she managed it for Monday's pole class.

Gabe hadn't texted her over the weekend, but that didn't worry her. She'd brought a little work home with her, and then while reading up on Greek mythology, she'd stumbled across a novel she'd enjoyed in college, and decided to reread it too. And then, given the chatter about strength training and nutrition in the divorced ladyfriends group chat, she'd decided to do a bit of meal planning in advance of the week, to make sure she was getting enough protein to help grow her new muscles. If she was going to put in enough work to make one or two servings of a chicken stir-fry with vegetables, she might as well make enough to eat all week.

Bringing some work home had meant a bit more flex time in her office hours, and so Kaity was able to successfully avoid Georgia for one whole day. She would take the wins wherever she could, even if it meant working alone at home, "home" being the apartment that she was still settling into, and that honestly still felt a little lonely.

She'd done her best to decorate, though interior design wasn't her strong suit (funnily enough, when she told people her job was as an instructional designer, they occasionally mixed it up with being an interior designer, and she would get random questions about curtains until she corrected the misunderstanding). One reason that decorations were sparse was that her wedding album and assorted framed photos were at the bottom of a trunk under her bed, and she hadn't gotten around to buying more art for the walls.

Dating an artist might help address her empty walls. Or simply hanging out with an artist on friendly terms, Kaity mentally corrected herself.

Her home was still nice, primarily because it was her own space...it was just very quiet sometimes.

Going to Snapdragon meant being surrounded by people again, and by the time early evening rolled around, Kaity was ready for it. She put on sweatpants over the bicycle shorts, and drove the few miles there.

Everyone knew that it was climb day, and so the faces in the mirror during Jenny's aerobic warm-up were equal parts intense and frightened. The sweats and joggers came off, and they ran through their existing move repertoire before Jenny began explaining the theory of pole climbs.

"This first move is a diagnostic, to help make sure you've got good placement and won't hurt your knee. Pick a foot," she instructed, "and put the front of your foot against the back of the pole. Your foot can be flexed for now to give you more grip, but eventually you'll have to learn to point it. Once your shin comes into contact with the pole, make sure that the pole is touching the inside of your knee, not the kneecap itself. Start to lean into it. Lean forward and grasp the pole with both hands, and see if you can lift the other foot off the ground for a second. It's a bit like doing a pull-up towards the pole." She demonstrated, and made it look effortless, as though she had simply glued one foot to the pole while the other hovered in a graceful bend.

Kaity exchanged nervous looks with Anabelle, and then pressed the top of her right foot to the side of the pole closest to her. The pole was cold. And hard. She leaned in and grabbed the pole with both hands, and pushed off...and nothing happened.

She looked around the room. No one had managed lift-off at first, except for Miriam, who now looked like a gothic Christmas ornament suspended from a metal tree.

"Try it on the other side now," Jenny suggested cheerfully. Kaity tried, and so did everyone else, but there was not much progress for most of them. A dull burn began in her arms.

"All right, here's the actual climbing method," said Jenny, undeterred. "This time, don't try to hover, but immediately bring your other foot to the other side of the pole." Again, she demonstrated, by touching her left foot to the side of the pole closest to her, and then bracing with her hands, and then wrapping her right foot around the opposite side of the pole, so that the space between her heel and her calf was snugly fit around the pole. She lifted her hands away, and hung out for a few moments, only her legs on the pole.

"Wow," someone said to Kaity's right, probably Maricela.

"Does the placement of your hands matter?" Kaity asked.

"Great question, Kaity!" Jenny replied. Kaity had been impressed with how quickly Jenny had learned all of their names; she wouldn't have managed without Anabelle's help.

"Right now, in a basic climb, you can place your hands wherever is comfortable, but make sure not to have them too high, or too low." Jenny pantomimed why each extreme was a bad idea: with her hands too high and her arms fully extended, she hung limply from the pole, unable to use her arm strength to leverage her way into a climb. With her hands too low, by her belly button, she was also unable to use her arms to do much other than stay clamped onto the pole right where she was.

Jenny did a few more basic climbs from the ground to demonstrate ideal hand placement, and Kaity made a note that having one hand at face-height and the other hand slightly above that seemed to work well. Right or left on top did not seem to matter.

"All right, let's all give it a try!" Jenny announced, making it sound like she was everyone's personal cheerleader.

Kaity wrapped her hands around the pole again. This time she tried with her left foot in back of the pole, and then wrapped her right foot around the front. Her arm muscles strained, her thighs burned, and her feet hurt like hell, but she managed to ascend a little bit before releasing everything and dropping to the ground.

"Kaity, you nailed it!" Anabelle screeched. Kaity blushed in response.

Various members of class were calling out encouraging things to one another, so once that had calmed down, Jenny instructed them in the next step: holding the climb for longer, and relying on their legs to help them stay on the pole. Once that was feeling more natural, they could work on taking their hands off, and climbing even more.

It was hard, and Kaity suspected that she was beginning to bruise her ankles and shins, but she made a few more rudimentary climbs. More than once, she had to use the towels and spray bottles of alcohol provided by the studio to wipe down the pole and her hands, because she was starting to get really sweaty.

Class ended soon after, and Kaity pulled on her sweats and took a seat in the lobby while figuring out what was next. Miriam had bowed out of their loose dinner plans, citing an exam that she had to study for. Anabelle was in the bathroom, changing into what she described as "real-people clothes," and she had sounded hesitant about dinner before ducking in.

Her phone chirped. It was a text from Gabe: *you free?*
Just finished pole class, she messaged back.

Can I call? he replied. Kaity hesitated. This was less-frequent contact than people who were actively dating, she supposed, and more contact than relative strangers might have. It might be an innocuous request, or it might lead to something to distract her from her empty apartment.

She'd responded affirmatively when Anabelle emerged from the bathroom.

"Hey, so I'm out for dinner but I really wanted to ask you—" Anabelle began, just as Kaity's phone began ringing.

Kaity glanced apologetically at Anabelle and answered. "Hey," she said. Gabe said, "Hey" on the other end.

Anabelle walked over to the front desk.

"What are you up to tonight?" Gabe asked.

"Nothing really, I don't have any more work to do for the day."

Anabelle returned to where Kaity was sitting and put a flyer in front of her face. It was too close for Kaity to focus on.

"I was wondering if you wanted to—" Gabe started, while Kaity furiously shook her head at Anabelle. "Go away," she mouthed.

"—start a concept shoot. I have some robes that would double as costumes in my studio."

"Umm, hold on, Anabelle is trying to tell me something," Kaity said, both to stall for time and to figure out why Anabelle was being so insistent.

The flyer she was holding turned out to be an ad for class that started in two days and lasted seven weeks, and promised to take students through a sexy, slinky floor choreography with Sophia to be performed at the next showcase. Each subsequent word made Kaity's heart drop a bit more.

"I can't," she whispered.

"Why not?" Anabelle whispered back.

"Obviously I can't perform anything, I'm not good at this, and plus I need to get back to Gabe, I think he wants to shoot tonight and I don't know if I'm ready."

Kaity took her phone out of where she'd been holding it in her purse to muffle that exchange.

"Er, sorry, we're still at the pole studio."

"What do you think? We could also swap some childhood stories, the kinds of things that would make being each others' dates more convincing."

He had a point, Kaity noted. Even if the whole photoshoot thing seemed both implausible and scary.

Anabelle got her attention again by furiously tapping one line on the flyer: "For all levels," it read. Kaity still shook her head.

"I think I'm in," Kaity said, "but I don't know about shooting..."

More furious tapping by Anabelle. "Sexy," the ad promised. "Slinky." As though it could deliver even Kaity into the promised land of being a confident, unrepentantly sexy vixen.

Which...might actually be what she needed. She liked living alone and being alone, but maybe not forever. As she sat on the padded bench in the lobby, Kaity felt her thighs and calves throbbing from the exertion of learning to climb the pole. She wondered what it would be like to come home to someone who would gently undress her, kiss the reddened areas even where there was cellulite, and run playful fingertips along her skin. Maybe that someone didn't exist yet, or at all...but Kaity could begin to exist as her own someone, a confident and sexy someone.

"Okay," Kaity said to Gabe, nodding to show Anabelle that the affirmation was for her as well. "Okay, I'm in."

Gabe shifted enough props and stools and stands around in his studio for there to be space for a model to recline on the canvas backdrop that covered one wall and half the floor. He made sure the latticed upright screen was positioned well for someone to change in and out of a costume. He even turned the heat up, in case Kaity was cold.

She knocked quietly on his studio door right when she said she'd be there, and he let her in. Her cheeks were a little flushed, and he could see where the pinkness crept down her neck into what little her forest green shirt revealed of her chest. It was an appealing contrast.

He got the banter going, explaining that tonight wasn't about any high concept stuff, just getting comfortable shooting and figuring out if they wanted to go in certain directions or not. He suspected that she'd need a while to feel at ease with a camera, and besides, she would benefit from a little more prep before Easter dinner, which was coming up that weekend.

"So I've got the screen set up for you to change behind, and there are a few different robes for you to try on and see which fit." Gabe gestured, then stepped aside. Kaity nodded, and walked to the same chair where she'd sat last time. She set down her purse, and then stepped out of her shoes.

Gabe saw the bruises and couldn't help but respond.

"Is that from pole class?" he asked, pointing to her feet.

Kaity nodded, chagrin on her face. "Yeah, we learned to climb today."

Gabe moved closer and ushered her into the next chair over.

"Damn, you're a trooper, I don't think I could've done that," he said, kneeling to take a closer look.

Kaity stiffened and pulled her feet out of his hands.

"What are you doing?" she asked, her voice tight.

Gabe stayed on his knees but pulled back to make eye contact with her. Her hazel eyes were wide, and the former flush in her cheeks had vanished. He would normally characterize her face as gently rounded, with generous curves like the rest of her, but now her face appeared pinched, shuttered.

"I was just... I wanted to get you off your feet, since it looked like they hurt. I could bring some ice from the vending machine, or rub them for you."

Disbelief shone from her eyes. "You would...do that? For a stranger?"

Gabe stayed very still for a moment. Then, without moving much at all, he gently eased back another foot or so, staying on his knees before her.

"I've worked with models who've worn six-inch heels for hours. I had it easy compared to them, so once I got to know them, I rubbed their feet for them. It wasn't, like, a sex thing. It was just a nice thing to do."

Kaity's face eased, and Gabe found himself wondering what the hell had happened in her past. Well, they were only fake-dating; there was no reason he couldn't ask.

"Why...?" he paused, not sure which question to ask. He didn't want to upset her, but she already seemed upset.

She sighed. "This is stupid. But my ex-husband used to offer to rub my feet when he wanted sex. At first it was novel, and it helped get me in the mood. Then I realized it was the only way he knew how to try to do something I'd enjoy, because we'd drifted that far apart. And then the foot rubs stopped coming, because we'd continued drifting. I'm...not used to having my feet touched anymore."

Gabe took all this in and said, "Okay, maybe you're not in a good place to shoot tonight." What he really wanted to do was gather Kaity in his arms and comfort her, tell her that she was pretty and smart and worthy, generally worthy as a human being, of affection and all kinds of good things. But it wasn't his place to do that. Hell, he didn't even bring dates back to his place if he could help it, because his apartment was just somewhere he slept, not somewhere he was building a life.

He stood up, dragged a chair to sit across from her at a safe distance, and said, "How about we just keep getting to know each other? I'll tell you a funny story from when I was a kid, if you'll tell me one of yours." That earned a hesitant smile.

Two stories later—he'd told the one about almost getting arrested for trespassing because he wanted to reenact the Sesame Street movie *Don't Eat the Pictures*, and she'd told one about blurting out that Grandpa was raised in a barn, missing the distinction between farm and barn at a young age—he could tell that she was beginning to relax. If he'd wanted to, if he had no stake in how this turned out, he probably could've started flirting with her, and made at least decent progress before ending the night (whether or not it ended with them in bed; he could plant the seeds for a future hook-up).

But as Gabe smiled, and chatted, and dredged up another story (this one involving superglue), he found himself shying away from the idea of seducing Kaity just for the hell of it. She was interesting. She was cool. He could see himself becoming friends with her. Which was why it was a fantastic idea for them to fake-date and then call it off after all the high-stakes gigs, so they could go on being friends. It would be a good time: play-acting a bit of romance, then chilling like platonic buds.

Eventually, though, they would ideally get around to doing this shoot. Until Snapdragon had another showcase, Gabe didn't have anything artsy in the works, and he knew he'd need to scratch that itch sooner or later. And working stiffs like him couldn't just take off and do a residency in the middle of nowhere Maine, as much as he'd like to have the opportunity.

So when he walked Kaity to the door after a couple of hours had passed—those hours filled with laughter, smiles, and plenty of embarrassing stories—he asked if she would come back on Thursday. And when she said yes, he found that his answering smile was more genuine than any he could remember lately.

Chapter 12

K aity didn't sleep well that night. Or the next.

She'd returned home from Gabe's studio feeling alternately happy and frustrated: happy that she and Gabe had finally clicked and just hung out, enjoying each other's company, but frustrated because of the emotions that had come up during their first start-stop-stutter of the evening.

If she was honest with herself, she'd felt aroused. And then disgusted with herself, but moreso with John, because he'd trained her like one of Pavlov's fucking dogs to respond to a foot massage in an erotic way.

So she'd come home, brewed a cup of her most comforting herbal tea, and gotten out the old rabbit vibrator she kept for rare occasions when she just wanted physical pleasure.

Tired and out of willpower to try to pretend that she didn't find Gabe attractive, she fantasized about him backing her up against a wall, which would feel like when he backed her up against her car for a kiss on the cheek last week. Except it wouldn't just be a kiss on the cheek, it would be a deeper kiss, and he'd put his hands in her hair, and then into her blouse, and then keep moving them down...

Despite the release from her vibrator, Kaity still didn't sleep well. She tried not to overthink things and failed. More than anything, she worried about whether John was right: whether she was too irrevocably broken to be in a relationship again...even a fake relationship.

Work was thankfully uneventful, but there was something Kaity was dreading even more: the slinky sexy floorwork class with Sophia, which started on Wednesday night. And suddenly it was Wednesday.

She drove up to Snapdragon, rehearsing various ways to apologize and back out of it. *I'm too busy with work. This thing with Gabe is taking more time than I'd thought. Actually, I'm too broken and have too many weird hang-ups about sex to want to do anything labeled sexy, ever.* Maybe that last one didn't need to be said, just thought really loud.

What had she been thinking, agreeing to this? She had a dim memory of Anabelle shoving a flyer in her face at a time when she was flying high from the accomplishment of her first pole climb, and also planning to hang out with Gabe, and considering the possibility that maybe she could reinvent herself in a sexier light.

Kaity parked and rested her forehead on her steering wheel. The weak April evening light barely warmed her.

Someone tapped on her window, and Kaity started. It was Anabelle, wearing a grin and a maroon bodysuit.

Kaity opened her door.

"Are we doing this?" she asked wearily.

"Yep!" Anabelle replied. And that was that. If Kaity knew anything, it was that sitting still and refusing to do anything had led to stagnation in her marriage, and she couldn't risk that again. So off she went, for another new experience, silently reassuring herself that she didn't have to like it, she just had to try it.

The class was small, and Kaity couldn't decide if that was a good thing or a bad thing. It was her, Anabelle, and Miriam from the beginner cohort, and three other women Kaity didn't know. Sophia wore patterned leggings and glasses, which made her look more like a normal person and less like the confident vixen who'd seduced the audience on showcase night. Her long red hair was in a braid that hung down her back as she checked everyone in.

They were in Studio 3, a smaller studio to the left of the main lobby. There were only three poles in it; most of it was open dance floor.

"Welcome to Slinky Floorwork Choreography," Sophia said, smiling and making eye contact with everyone in turn. "The idea of this class is to learn a few basic movements, put them together in a choreography, and rehearse so that we can do a group routine at the next showcase in a couple months. This is an all-levels class, starting from the ground up, and you don't need to be proficient on a pole. I'm also hoping to teach some basics of performing: eye contact, stage presence, and all that other good stuff."

No one ran from the room screaming, though Kaity was sorely tempted. Sophia led them through a warm-up that was similar to Jenny's in that it was to pop music and got every part of the body warm, but Sophia's warm-up had a lot more hip circles, chest circles, and general circles. They went to their mats for a series of cat and cow yoga movements and related things. There were even some push-ups on their knees. Kaity didn't think she could manage push-ups, but to her surprise, she pounded them out. Pole dancing was apparently helping with her overall strength.

Once through with the warm-up, they put on knee-pads (Anabelle lent Kaity an old pair), and then they learned how to crawl...sexily. Sophia demonstrated a crawl, seeping across the floor in a liquid, languid fashion. Then she demonstrated a second crawl, which was somehow sassier, involving hair tosses, and not as low to the ground. Then Sophia named both crawls, explaining that these were the main two they would focus on in this choreography, but there were more. The part of Kaity's brain that automatically filed away new facts noted that there were more styles of crawl than she'd anticipated in pole-dance-and-adjacent dance styles.

Then it was time to try. All the students got down on their hands and knees, trying first the melty crawl and second the sassy crawl. At first Kaity felt like a toddler scooting across the floor, aiming for a juice box.

The kneepads meant it didn't hurt, but there was a lot of flailing nonetheless, accompanied by shame that this was yet another arena in which Kaity was failing at being sexy.

Sophia must have sensed her distress, because she came to Kaity's rescue.

"Okay—Kaity, right? —in the sassy crawl, you need to be able to tilt and tuck your hips in the different phases of the crawl. Can I put my hands on your hips to help you feel that motion?"

Close to tears, Kaity nodded.

She stayed on her hands and knees, and Sophia stood over her, gently reaching to place her hands on the sides of Kaity's hips, with her fingers wrapping into Kaity's belly and thumbs towards her spine. Sophia applied pressure with her thumbs to get Kaity to curl her hips inward—the tuck—and then pulled back more with her fingers to get Kaity to arch her lower back a bit—the tilt—uncurling her hips and arching her whole spine.

"Feel that?" Sophia asked.

Kaity nodded. "Tuck, curl in," she whispered, doing the motion herself. "Tilt, push out." And she did that too.

"Good! Looks like you've got it! Now to start the sassy crawl, tilt your hips, and pull your hips back until you're almost all the way back in a child's pose. That will tuck your hips. Thread a knee through, move your arms to the side, move your other leg so your hips come to the ground, push back in a tilt, and repeat—yes, that's it!"

Kaity felt her spine contracting and extending, and she was able to begin to travel with the crawl. The rule Sophia had given them was to thread your right knee if you wanted to travel to the right, and your left knee if you wanted to travel to the left. So she started in one direction, doubled back for a few crawls, and resumed forward motion. She caught a glimpse of herself in the mirror, and she didn't look like crap. She crawled til she was almost on the mirror, then rolled to one side to sit. Anabelle and Miriam were still struggling with the move, but the other three women seemed to have a handle on it; they were probably more advanced students.

"All right everyone, time for a quick break," Sophia announced. "Grab some water, and we'll run the drill again with a new twist."

Grateful for the water break, Kaity rolled out her wrists. Sophia called them all back to the dance floor, and explained the next drill: half of them would sassy crawl at a time, with the other half seated as their audience at the far end of the room. Each crawler would have one audience member sitting by the wall...and the goal was to make, and maintain, eye contact.

"It might feel awkward at first," Sophia cautioned them, "but this is practice for performing, and feeling comfortable in your own skin."

Unlikely, Kaity thought, before getting caught up in worrying who she'd be paired with. She could probably manage the exercise with Anabelle, but she had her doubts about even that.

Sophia pointed Kaity towards one of the other women in the class, Nina. She appeared to be a little older than Kaity, and she wore neon green shorts and a matching sports bra that contrasted with her dark skin. Seeming to sense Kaity's nervousness, she smiled and offered to go first.

Kaity nestled her back against the studio wall, and Sophia dimmed the lights and put on some music. It was slow, but still with a pulsing rhythm. Across the studio, Nina knelt, staring off in another direction. Then she tilted her hips and pushed back, starting the sassy crawl towards Kaity. When not in the middle of changing directions, she managed to gaze at Kaity, with an open, easy smile on her face. As she felt out the move, she began to incorporate a hair toss while switching from one side of the crawl to the other, sending her braids flying.

The prolonged eye contact made Kaity squirm a little, because it was so intense. But it was also fun to watch, and it felt just a tad illicit, like she was being invited to witness something private, something not for public consumption. Then Nina stopped, and Kaity realized it was because Nina had almost landed on top of her with her last crawl.

A tad out of breath, Nina said, "That was intense." Kaity nodded, and said, "Sorry for all the awkwardness you're about to witness." That got a chuckle out of Nina, and then Kaity waited for a signal from Sophia to stand and join the other two dancers at the far wall.

She knelt to the ground, got on her hands and knees, and tried to spend a moment just breathing. She imagined Sophia's hands gently guiding her hips to tilt and tuck, remembering the sensations of it, how it felt in her body. Then she tilted her hips to push back, starting the sassy crawl. It took her a crawl or two to remember that she was supposed to be looking at Nina.

At first Kaity blinked a lot to break up the eye contact. But each time she looked at Nina, she was the same: calm and smiling. Kaity's hair fell into her eyes and she tossed her head to clear her vision, happening to do so at a particularly good moment in the crawl, when the hair toss punctuated the end of one crawl and the beginning of another.

"Yes, get it!" Sophia crowed, and Kaity felt herself begin to giggle. She looked at Nina, and Nina started laughing too, and then Kaity had finished the floor drill and practically collapsed in Nina's lap.

"First time with this drill, huh?" Nina asked. Kaity grimaced and nodded. "You'll get there," Nina said. "We all do eventually."

Apart from the unpleasant realization that this class was two hours long, since they had a lot of material to cover before the next showcase, Kaity didn't have as bad a time as she'd feared. There was something oddly cathartic about crawling and rolling around on the ground. After some more moves and drills, they'd sat and stretched, and talked about the show itself. With six performers—seven if Sophia joined—they had a number of options for how to arrange their choreography. Given that Sophia has chosen a song that was only two minutes long, a sensual cover of "Tainted Love," the proposition of memorizing and performing a choreography was less daunting than it'd initially seemed.

Also, with Kaity's deadline to decide if she was leaving M-town coming up, going a little outside her comfort zone didn't scare her as much as it usually did. It's not like she'd ever see any of these people ever again.

"Sooo, what did you think?" Anabelle asked after class. They'd said goodbye to Miriam and the others, and were sitting in Kaity's car to chat for a few moments while avoiding the evening chill.

"I thought it'd be a lot worse," Kaity confessed. "I don't know what I'm doing half the time, and I feel like an ungainly infant, but it's actually kinda fun."

"That's what I thought too!" Anabelle beamed. "Okay, well, I've gotta dash, see you soon." Kaity waved, and made a mental note to text Anabelle later to see if she needed any more help after hours. If Kaity was bad at asking for help, Anabelle was even worse.

After starting her car, Kaity saw that someone had texted her.

It was Gabe: *Easter this weekend, you up for meeting one of my old buddies tomorrow? We can all compare notes on dealing with my family.*

Kaity definitely found herself curious about Gabe's family and friends. She responded in the affirmative.

Great, how about you, me, and Alex meet at the Tap District at 7? Kaity agreed, and wondered if she was about to meet yet another bohemian artist type. If so, maybe he'd have some insights into how Gabe worked ...just so she could play her role better, of course.

Chapter 13

Gabe and Alex grabbed a table at the Tap District a little before 7. It was a Thursday night, so not overly crowded, but the place filled to capacity most weekends, and it seemed like tonight's business was moving in that direction.

Gabe spotted Kaity as she walked in hesitantly, and called her name, waving.

"She's cute," Alex murmured.

"Hands off," Gabe muttered back, referencing the old joke that they always went for the same girls, even though they'd never actually dated the same woman.

"Hi," Kaity said as she pulled up a chair. They were at a high-top, around the edges of the restaurant. In the center was a large rectangular bar, with beer taps lining the interior island in all directions. TV screens also hung from the bar, broadcasting multiple sports games between them all.

"This is Alex," Gabe said, and Alex stretched out a hand for Kaity to shake. Kaity only paused a moment before grasping and shaking.

"Nice to meet you," she said, followed by, "I thought you would be a guy."

Alex preened. Her sandy blond hair was pulled up in a high ponytail, and when standing, she was as tall as Gabe. She wore an outfit that would look at home at a rock concert: a faded T-shirt and ripped jeans.

"Told you I liked this one," Alex said to Gabe. "She's honest, and you could use some of that in your life, to cut through the bullshit your family piles on."

Kaity took a seat and tried to follow their banter. It was clear that they'd been friends for a very long time, and that Alex wasn't a big fan of Gabe's family. As they ordered drinks—beers for Gabe and Alex, a cider for Kaity—Gabe tried to steer the conversation towards Easter in particular.

"Okay so, Easter dinner is a big deal in my family," Gabe said.

"It's true!" Alex affirmed. "One time I showed up straight from soccer practice, and Gabe's mom made me change into a dress. Er, step-mom," she corrected herself, after a glare from Gabe.

"My step-mom, Marcia," Gabe said, "is really into celebrating the holidays. And she married my dad right around Easter, so it kinda became associated with their anniversary." For a second, he wondered why he was giving Kaity all this insight into his messed-up family. Ever since his mom's death, everything had felt wrong. And Marcia had tried to fill all the right gaps in all the wrong ways, or maybe all the wrong gaps in all the right ways. His dad was certainly into her, and bought all her bullshit about wanting them to be a big, happy family together. Holly's birth had just cemented all that.

"Tell her the best part," Alex urged. Gabe's eyes shot to Kaity, and he saw her eyes widen. Probably in fear, he thought glumly. Which wasn't entirely unwarranted. This was the part of his life that was messy, even for an artist.

Gabe clasped his hands painfully tight atop the table, and looked down at them. The veins in the backs of his hands stood out, like they always did when he was stressed or overworked.

"After my mom died, and Marcia married my dad, and Holly was born...I ran away from home." Gabe stared at the wooden tabletop rather than meet Kaity's eyes. "Nothing bad happened, I still managed to finish high school, and then I moved to the East Coast for art school. But Marcia assumed I'd be a bad influence on her kid, and so she said, and I quote, 'you are never to set foot in this house again, except for holidays, until you clean up your act.'"

Alex chortled at the phrasing and the disapproving tone they'd spent years secretly mocking. Gabe finally met Kaity's eyes. Clearly she was taking it all in. At least she didn't have her notebook out. He drew a breath and decided to continue.

"It's not like I was doing much in the way of drugs or alcohol. But somehow she got it in her head that I was a bad kid and would always be one, so there's no way I'd be anything other than a bad influence on her pre-cious daughter." Even though Holly was his half-sister, for God's sake, and Gabe should be there for her, to help counterbalance the hoity-toity socialization Marcia was no doubt shoving down her throat.

Kaity sipped her cider, clearly gathering her thoughts.

"And you want me to help you win her over, right?" she asked.

"I guess you could put it like that," Gabe answered.

"What does she like? What should I talk to her about?" The questions were so obvious that Gabe felt stupid for not having an immediate answer. He'd just been a kid when Marcia had entered their lives, and what kid cared about their parent's hobbies? But he realized that he had never really taken the time to get to know his step-mom when he'd become an adult, either.

Luckily, Alex fielded that one. "She's super into charity groups and volunteer work, since they have enough money and Gabe's dad is retired now. Oh my god, Gabe, remember that time when she tried to get us to volunteer at that Thanksgiving fundraiser when we were in high school, but we were too hungover to show up?"

Kaity coughed to cover a laugh, then smiled. "Volunteering, got it. I can work with that."

Gabe scowled into his beer and made an attempt to steer the conversation back into territory he knew he could contribute something to. "They also go to church at the big Presbyterian church on Meridian. We're just lucky we're not getting dragged to services too."

With that, the conversation turned to religion, and how all three of them were some flavor of non-religious people, after having been raised by parents who were overzealous about the supposed positive impact of Sunday school. Kaity seemed to roll with it all, though Gabe wasn't sure if Kaity was ready for the hot mess that was his family.

"Can I walk you to your car?" Gabe asked after they'd settled up. He'd insisted on treating Kaity to her beverage; doing something nice for her gave him a warm little glow. Kaity, after standing up and putting her purse over her shoulder, nodded. She smiled and waved to Alex, and then caught up to where Gabe was holding the restaurant's door open.

He shortened his stride at first, since her legs were shorter than his, but then he noticed a slight...shift. Not quite a limp. When they reached her car, he asked, "Hey, are you okay?"

She laughed heartily, one of the least restrained gestures he'd ever seen from her. "Sure, I mean, it sounds like I'm walking into a bit of a trap on Easter, and I'm sore from this new slinky choreo class, and I might be leaving—" She cut herself off. "It's just...been a weird day for you to ask that question."

They reached her car. Gabe knew better than to try to reach out and touch her, soothe her, since that might inspire a bad reaction like last time. So he willed himself to stillness and asked, "Can I do anything to help?"

This time, her laugh was a bit unsteady. She looked around the parking lot, at everything but him. "It's weird, but I wouldn't say no to a massage this time." Gabe's eyebrows lifted, and he kept them there until he knew that she'd seen his expression.

"I am pretty decent at it, or so I'm told," he said.

Kaity was silent for a heartbeat. "Look, this was nice. But I think I'm going straight home and to bed. We could practice the cheek kiss thing, though."

She was standing with her side to her car, and Gabe didn't want to seem too aggressive, so he just stepped in to close the space between them. He stretched his arms around her, encircling her back, and lowered his lips to her cheek. While he was there, he lingered a moment, and he felt her hips faintly flex into him, and then away.

When he pulled back, she was blushing. "Um, yeah, dance moves from today. Still practicing. Gotta practice." She spun and started unlocking her car, leaving Gabe to respectfully back away and wonder what had just happened. He also tried to quash the memory of Kaity's hips curling into him, since that clearly was not the sort of thing fake boyfriends were supposed to dwell on. Cheek kisses and nothing more.

Chapter 14

E aster Sunday arrived.

Gabe hadn't answered Kaity's texts the night before, which she found a little upsetting, so she'd invited Anabelle over for a wardrobe consult and they'd spent half that time drinking wine and complaining about flaky people.

"Like, my god, he's the one who invited me to this Easter dinner," Kaity said, a glass of Pinot Grigio dangling from one hand while she gesticulated with the other. "And he can't be bothered to pick up his damn phone if I need to double check some stuff?"

"Girl, preach," Anabelle had averred. She'd switched to water so she could drive home, but she was clearly taking her role as emotional support clothier seriously. She had brought over some outfits she thought might fit Kaity, and had also loaded several tabs on her tablet with various spring fashion trends. The outfit they had settled on straddled the line between age-appropriate, comfortable, and just a little flirty, which seemed about right for Kaity's role in all this.

Getting to hang out with Anabelle just to mess around with clothes, hold a mini-fashion-show, and complain about men was fun...it was one of the things Kaity had missed out on while trying to make her marriage work. She'd had high hopes for becoming friends with Georgia, but, well, look how that had turned out.

Those thoughts were depressing enough that even after Anabelle had left, Kaity stayed up a while longer. She knew she'd be a bit sleep-deprived the next day, but she didn't know how to settle down for the night in a bed full of regrets.

Still, the next day arrived, bringing with it a mild headache. Kaity tugged on a floral skirt with a ruffled top and quietly resented the inexorable march of time. Closer to her deadline to move back to Louisville was both good and bad. The armbands of the shirt felt a tad tight, and she supposed that pole was to blame, since the numbers on the scale hadn't gone up.

She'd always thought silver looked a bit better on her than gold, but Gabe had given her a tiny gold flower pendant as an "early anniversary" gift, so she put it on, and found some gold studs in her jewelry box to match. Minimal makeup, because she was aiming for a natural look, and then she slid on flats, hoping for no visible bruising on her feet and ankles, and waited for Gabe.

He first texted *sorry missed your texts, phone died*. Kaity was not sure what to do with that one. Then Gabe texted that he was on his way, and then he texted when he had arrived at her apartment complex. She'd asked him to, so that she had a sense of the timeline, and he had complied. She was grateful; being able to make small requests and not have them thrown back in her face as irrefutable evidence of her omnipresent anxiety was refreshing. Even if she was still annoyed that he hadn't been responsive the night before.

She stepped outside of the gate to meet him, and was the tiniest bit pleased when he stepped around to open the car door for her.

Once settled inside, Kaity turned to look at Gabe. He was in a plain white collared shirt and gray slacks. The sparse style suited him; his brown curls glowed in contrast.

"You look nice," he said.

"You too," she replied.

Kaity folded her hands during the drive, and watched as they navigated Mariontown neighborhoods she hadn't seen before. She guessed that they were somewhere on the northeast side of town, definitely northeast of Broad River, but by how much, it was anyone's guess. She'd seen so much more of M-town in the last few weeks, it'd be a shame to leave it...but her deadline was approaching. If her life wasn't significantly better than her pre-divorce life, she might as well go back to Louisville where she at least had more of a social and support network.

Eventually they turned down a street in the 70s range (Kaity didn't quite catch it...74th? 75th?) and then Gabe turned up a driveway with white picket fences lining it. They went up a slight incline, landing at a large circular driveway. There were already half a dozen cars parked in various locations.

As Gabe parked, Kaity turned towards him, with frantic feelings belatedly setting in. What was she doing here? What was this weird arrangement?

"I—we—" she started.

He leaned across the console and kissed her. Kaity's panicky inhale settled into something deeper and in rhythm with Gabe's breathing. This is nice, she thought. Their lips fit together nicely, and he kept it tame, not going tongue-spelunking. But the skin-to-skin contact, and the fresh smell of his aftershave, it was all quite unexpected and quite nice.

Gabe pulled away, and Kaity managed not to whimper a protest.

"I hope that was okay," he said. Kaity nodded. "My uncle just walked by and I know he reports directly to my mom." She nodded again, trying to even out her breathing.

Gabe got out and opened the door for her, and Kaity praised past-Kaity who'd chosen to wear flats; otherwise, she might have been a little wobbly. Gabe extended an arm to her; in his other hand was the requisite bouquet.

"Okay, so remember our signal," he was saying. "If you need me to bail you out, like if they're quizzing you on something you can't bluff your way through, call me over to talk about our photoshoot, which is on Greek mythology. If it's a red alert, like you need to be bailed out immediately, then go to Roman mythology."

Kaity nodded resolutely. They walked past manicured bushes and up a brick path to the front door.

The door, with an impressive array of glass cut-outs in it, swung open as they approached.

A late-middle-aged woman in a sternly cut but brightly colored dress looked them over, and then nodded. "Good, you're here on time. Gabe, who is your friend?"

"Hi, Marcia," Gabe responded, and Kaity noticed that his jaw was clenching ever so slightly. "This is Kaity. We've been dating for about two months now and as I said over text, I'd really like for you all to meet her."

Looking closely, though Kaity knew Marcia and Gabe weren't biologically related, she thought she could identify a stubborn cast to both their jaws. Marcia's face was more oval in shape than Gabe's, lined with wrinkles that indicated time more time spent frowning than smiling. Kaity resolved to be as gracious as possible, regardless of how much Marcia was the bad guy in this situation.

"It's nice to meet you," Kaity said promptly. "Thank you for inviting us. We brought flowers for the table." Marcia smiled minutely at that, and ushered them in.

Gabe had described his parents as having a wasteful amount of money, which they then put into wasteful, soulless decorating. Kaity could certainly see how he'd arrived at that conclusion: all the rooms of the house were on the large side of practical, and the attempts at homey touches—picture frames, wall hangings—seemed inadequate at translating a house into a home. As she met the rest of the family—Gabe's father Ron, his younger sister Holly, and a handful of aunts and uncles—Kaity smiled and charmed her way through it, beginning to understand why Gabe's freewheeling and artistic nature might put him at odds with the rest of his family, status-oriented as they seemed.

The flowers did indeed go onto the table, but they were dwarfed by the large and obviously expensive bouquets that already acted as centerpieces. Kaity offered to help with the food, and was half-surprised, half-relieved to have her offer accepted, since she'd begun to suspect that Gabe's family hired help up to and including dinner staff.

In the kitchen, which sported a gigantic marble island, Marcia seemed only minimally curious about Kaity as they started to put the appetizers into serving dishes.

"How did you two meet?" Marcia asked, arranging deviled eggs on a scalloped crystal platter.

"Oh, at a dance studio on the northside," Kaity responded. "I take classes there, and Gabe was consulting about a photoshoot." The aroma of the ham-asparagus bundles and caprese-stuffed mushrooms was starting to make her mouth water.

"What sort of dance?"

"P—" and Kaity's brain stuttered, realizing pole dance might be seen as inappropriate, "p—ilates." She smiled, pleased at pulling the conversation out of the fire, and silently thanking Anabelle for her penchant for trying new fitness classes and dragging Kaity along to them. Were there many other dance styles that started with a P? Would she even have them at the tip of her tongue? Was there any Polynesian dance in the Midwest to speak of?

"I've been meaning to try that," Marcia mused. "Keeping one's figure while one's age advances is rather challenging. Do you like the classes there?"

"Oh yes, very much," Kaity replied, glad that she was able to be honest about one thing. If the aromas were any indication, though, she would be able to honestly compliment Marcia's cooking and attempt to bond with the woman over a shared love of food.

Everyone behaved over the meal, and once they were into the main course, everyone had questions for Kaity about her job and how she liked Mariontown. She linked hands with Gabe between courses, and attempted an Anabelle-worthy enthusiastic smile the whole time. Iced tea during the meal and coffee with dessert ensured that she had to go find the bathroom at least once; it was an obnoxiously teal affair that, though large, left Kaity feeling claustrophobic. She came away from the meal with an enhanced understanding of what Gabe didn't like about his family—overt financial privilege, poor design choices, a tendency to talk over him when he talked about his life and art—but she also came to realize that family drama probably always looked and felt worse from the inside. Holly was cute as a button, and clearly thrilled to have her older brother to interact with, so as the gathering ended, Kaity was genuinely glad that she'd agreed to be Gabe's arm candy. He deserved that time with his family, that sense of love and belonging, even if it was mainly with one family member rather than the whole of them.

Kaity just hoped her own upcoming gathering would go half as well.

Chapter 15

Gabe was animated on the ride home, talking about how he'd connected with Holly over schoolwork (they'd had the same awful chemistry teacher) and sports. He sounded excited, and Kaity loved to hear it in his voice.

When they reached her apartment, buoyed by the feeling of actually pulling this off and wanting more, Kaity invited him up. "For that massage," she said, feeling bold. For once, she felt on top of the world: she was taking dance classes that scared her, she'd met his scary stepmother, and she'd held it together the whole time. Best of all, none of this mattered: if Kaity left town, this would all be a distant memory, and she could get on with her life, even if she messed something up.

Kaity led him up the stairs, making one awkward joke about how she'd seen his home, so now it was only fair that he see hers.

As usual, her apartment was tidy. She gave him a perfunctory tour, and invited him to sit on the loveseat, while she pulled up a chair. They'd just eaten a rich meal, so she offered to make tea.

Kaity returned from the kitchen and found Gabe up and moving around. Not exactly what she had anticipated, but he did seem like a curious person. He was snooping around her books, and the handful of photos she had up.

"Here," she said, extending a mug to him. He turned to face her, smiling, and once again she had to admit to herself that she found his smile dazzling.

He returned to the loveseat, and she sat nearby.

"So...that seemed to go well?" she ventured.

"Oh yes," he said, blowing on his mug of tea. "I think I'm going to get an invite to Holly's next soccer game. It seemed like Marcia liked you, and my dad congratulated me on finally finding a nice woman to date. Not that I necessarily trust his taste in women, but you know."

Kaity drew back a little bit, feeling insulted but not quite sure why. She began to doubt herself, her plan to get a massage and maybe a little more, since it had seemed like Gabe was maybe judging her right then. Or his dad was? But then he agreed with his dad?

"So, about this massage..." Gabe said, setting his mug down on the coffee table and leaning forward. "Do you want to tell me where to begin?"

Fighting down ambivalence, Kaity paused to assess: her feet were definitely off-limits, for now at least. But she'd done a lot of standing during the day, and her flats, while better than heels, weren't the most supportive shoes in her wardrobe.

"Calves?" she suggested. She'd kicked off her shoes when entering her home, as she always did, so she was already sitting barefoot, her peach-painted toenails faintly winking in the dim light.

Gabe lifted his hands and squared his posture towards her, so that she could deposit her feet in his lap, poking more towards his back hence slightly out of reach. The fact that he remembered that she'd had an adverse reaction to having her feet touched was a plus, she grudgingly admitted.

He dropped his hands onto one shin, running them lightly up and down the skin for a few strokes. Then he migrated them to the underside, the pads of his fingertips exploring the softer folds of muscle.

"I haven't gotten my hands on a pole dancer yet," Gabe mused. "Feels like a lot of muscle in the calf? I'm assuming you spend a lot of time on the balls of your feet?"

Kaity, who was starting to slouch in her chair with relaxation and pleasure, managed a soft, "Mm-hmm."

Gabe stopped talking but kept exploring, and she felt him drag oodles of tension from her calves—her right calf, to be specific—and knead away the stress of the day. Then he switched to her left leg. For once, she could just relax and lean into a sensation that felt good: no ex-husband nagging her about how she was broken, no ex-sister-in-law plaguing her, no work, just play.

"Does this feel okay?" Gabe asked, interrupting Kaity's reverie.

"Yes," she managed to murmur. "It's great, don't stop."

He kept going, and once he'd worked that calf, he begin to massage gently around the kneecap, and then up onto her left quad. Kaity reached down to help tug her floral skirt up a bit—she didn't think she was exposing anything by doing so—and then continued to enjoy the sensations of Gabe's hands working on her legs. He switched to the right thigh, and she continued to marinate in the bliss of it.

The sensation suddenly stopped.

Kaity opened her eyes, and to reorient herself, found her cup of tea and took a sip.

"Do you want me to keep going?" Gabe asked. He was leaning in slightly, brown curls dusting his forehead.

She nodded. "It feels really good." Then she paused, castigating herself for vague language. "What I mean is...it feels great. I can't remember the last time I got a massage. And my calves were definitely sore." She let a smile reach her lips, hoping that it came across as genuine, since it felt that way on her end.

"Should I stay with the calves, or...?" Gabe let the question dangle.

Kaity gathered her courage, pulled her feet back, and then clambered into Gabe's lap, straddling him. Being atop his lap brought her face almost on level with his, and she put her hands around his shoulders.

Gabe's eyes widened with surprise.

"I could use a scalp massage," Kaity breathed, her face inches from his. She'd let her hair down after making tea, and she hoped it looked good cascading around her shoulders. Gabe shifted slightly under her, freeing his hands, and he lifted his hands to gently touch her scalp right around her temples. Kaity closed her eyes and shuddered slightly.

"Is this okay?" he asked.

"I just got a chill," Kaity said. Which was true, in a way; the sensation was so new—or so old, because it'd been so long since she'd been with someone—but she also recognized an emotion that went with it.

Fear.

Fear that she would begin to care about Gabe, and he'd turn out to be just like her ex. Or she'd start to care about him, and then she'd leave because it was best for her career. Or she'd start to care about him, and...and...what if it simply worked?

Gabe had started caressing her hair again, running fingertips through the crown of her hair, and softly making swirling gestures against her scalp. It felt so good that it began to scare Kaity how much she wanted it, how much she wanted him.

Kaity felt her heart constrict. There was no way this would work. It was better to keep it to just-friends and pretend-partners. She started to pull back.

She met Gabe's eyes, and they were wide and curious. She managed a smile, and continued to pull back.

"Thank you for the massage," she said, easing back into her seat.

"Just a friendly massage?" Gabe asked, a hint of something in his voice that Kaity couldn't identify.

"Like the first time we hung out," she said. "You good with that?"

He nodded. "One event down, and one to go. Best idea all year. We've got this," and he grinned wryly.

He finished his tea in one gulp, and then stood up.

"Hang out again before your work party, yeah?" Kaity nodded, and saw him to the door.

As she collected the tea cups, Kaity mused that she seemed to need more touch in her life. Something about dancing regularly and having to touch herself and be touched in class was making her crave touch. She recalled being fine with long periods of being single earlier in her life, before marriage, but it felt different now. Like something in her was waking up, unfurling.

Maybe eventually she'd find someone who was right for her in the long term.

Gabe walked back to his car, a little unsettled and aroused. Kaity had come along to meet his neurotic family, played her part beautifully, and then actually climbed into his lap.

And then climbed right back out.

He didn't think she was playing hard to get. Kaity seemed overly honest, if a bit reserved. Maybe she didn't know what she wanted? She'd mentioned a few details from her divorce that made it sound like a painful time.

Which, again, was a shame. She was lovely to look at, fantastic to talk to, and nice to touch. She didn't seem prone to drama, which of course was a massive improvement over what a lot of his fellow artist friends got themselves wrapped up in. One of the couples a few doors down from him in the McMurphy had regular shouting matches, so much so that Gabe had resolved to try to never overlap his gallery walk hours with theirs.

But if she kept the mixed messages coming, he wasn't sure what he'd do. Would he sweep her off her feet and then maybe regret it later, when their totally different personalities inevitably clashed? Would he ignore her advances like he had tonight (well, somewhat) and then maybe miss out on a good time? He wasn't looking for anything serious, and it seemed like she didn't know what she was looking for at all.

Gabe looked at his phone. Easter Sunday meant some places would be closed, but he was already in SoBro, which boded well for hitting the strip in Broad River and finding some places filled with holiday orphans like himself. Come to think of it, Ian had mentioned holding court at the cocktail bar that had recently opened in that area.

Either way, the night was young, and whether he ended up in a bar or in a bed, he'd land on his feet. He always did.

Chapter 16

K aity walked into Snapdragon for her Monday pole class in a bit of a daze.

She had gone to work feeling out of it, and hadn't registered half the barbs Georgia had thrown her way. She simply went into her office during her lunch break, closed the door, and laid on the floor, tilting and tucking her hips. It was a weird sort of grounding exercise, but it felt like it might hold some answers for her: why she'd been so brazenly flirty with Gabe and then pulled back, for example.

She concluded that intimacy sounded nice, especially now that it felt like her body was waking up after being dormant. But maybe the idea of intimacy was nicer than the reality, and that was an okay thing to accept too.

After Jenny's usual warm-up, she talked them through a new move: the slinky.

Kaity and Anabelle exchanged amused looks, and then watched Jenny demonstrate the move, facing the pole with her feet close to it, and grasping it with her hands around the height of her neck. She led with her head, and then rolled the motion down her entire spin e...just like a slinky.

Kaity tried it, feeling awkward, and perked up as Jenny dispensed advice that had to do with the hips. They would start in a neutral position, then as the chest came in towards the pole to start the slinky-like rolling-down-the-spine motion, the hips would tuck, and then tilt as the roll-down continued.

To her delight and surprise, she got the slinky on her next try. Then, to her embarrassment, her imagination spun up an image of her holding onto Gabe instead of the pole, and her chest grazing him until she rolled her spine down, tucking and tilting through her hips. She took a break from practicing to shake out her forearms and grab some water, reflecting that pole sometimes seemed sensual and other times more like sporty exercise hell, and maybe that was just the kind of dance form it was.

Next, they brushed up on their climbs, and Kaity finally made some progress on hanging out in the upright sit without sliding to the ground. She knew it was bruising her calves, but then, her calves had been massaged so nicely yesterday, they didn't seem to mind the maltreatment.

As a whole class, they put the slinky into the routine they'd been learning, and Jenny announced that they would spend the next week rehearsing, so they could "perform" it for each other the final week of class.

"How are we almost through this class?" Kaity asked Anabelle as they gathered their things.

"Right?!" Anabelle replied. "What do you think about signing up for the next series?"

Kaity ducked her head, under the pretense of wrangling her shoes and socks. Her deadline to decide whether she was staying or going was approaching, and unless her work situation improved, going was the logical choice. She didn't feel like she'd made a lot of friends in the meantime, and getting entangled with Gabe in any real sense was clearly too risky.

"I feel a little overloaded being in two classes a week right now since the performance class is still going on," Kaity said, glad she was able to dredge up an honest answer.

"Well, think about it and let me know," Anabelle said. "Oh, Miriam!" and she waved down the younger woman. "Dinner tonight?"

Miriam straightened up from putting on black strappy sandals with chunky heels. "Sure. Did you guys have a place in mind?"

Kaity had prepared for this very question.

"I've heard good things about the Broad River Brewpub. They have both omnivorous and vegetarian options, and I've been wanting to check it out." Miriam and Anabelle agreed to meet there. As Kaity was getting into her car, she saw a text from Gabe, and decided to ignore it, in favor of living in the moment. During the short drive into Broad River, she ran through the pole sequence in her head, and then switched to the slinky choreo, even though they'd only learned a snippet of it.

Despite the weird mood Kaity had been in all day, she enjoyed her dinner company. She ordered a meatloaf sandwich, feeling like she'd earned her protein and carbs. Anabelle got a burger, and Miriam got the seitan reuben. They shared a plate of roasted root vegetables, which showed up in thick slices, glistening with brushed olive oil and glittering with salt.

Anabelle provided the social glue, bridging the obvious differences between the three of them. Kaity alternated sips of iced tea with bites of beet and potato, listening to Miriam talk about her life as the granddaughter of East European Jewish immigrants in the Midwest. She was back in school for a second bachelor's degree, aiming for a career in art therapy after a flirtation with biology. Anabelle talked about her move down from Chicago—married at first, then divorced, much like Kaity's story—and Anabelle also talked about her work with the immigrant center near where she lived. She had traveled to Europe multiple times too, sparking Miriam's interest since Anabelle had visited some of the places that Miriam's family had emigrated from.

To her surprise, Kaity found parts of her life unspooling conversationally. She talked about growing up in Louisville, how her family used to be close but drifted as everyone acquired their own adult values. She reminisced about college—and they all took turns commiserating with Miriam, who was *still* a student in her late twenties—and even talked a little about her marriage and her divorce.

Miriam listened attentively, and it dawned on Kaity that Miriam probably didn't see herself as the cool girl or mean girl that she gave off vibes as. It had never occurred to Kaity that someone like Miriam might see herself as an outsider—being Jewish in the Midwest, among other reasons—and just lean into it. Kaity had always craved acceptance, so the idea of standing out on purpose was foreign to her. But from Miriam's perspective, getting to hang out with some worldly older women was probably pretty cool. And the fact that they'd met at the pole dance studio was also pretty cool.

"So, why did you all start pole classes?" Miriam asked.

"Well, *she* dragged me in," Kaity said, gesturing to Anabelle with a sweet potato fry.

Anabelle blew Kaity a kiss. "Psh, you liked it! I don't know if you'd leave your apartment for anything but work if I didn't take you places, along with the other divorced ladyfriends." Kaity had to acknowledge the truth of that, even as Anabelle launched into an explanation of their social group and the resulting group chat. Anabelle concluded her definition of the divorced ladyfriends, and asked Miriam why she started coming to Snapdragon.

Miriam—to Kaity's surprise—blushed. "This is dumb, but I realized that I never got to show off my thigh tattoos. I thought pole dancing seemed cool, so I decided to give it a shot."

"Well, that's not any weirder of a reason than why I ended up there," Kaity said. People were just full of surprises, weren't they?

The meal progressed, the check came, and Anabelle swooped it up, saying she'd just gotten paid.

"All right, but it's my turn next," said Kaity. "And Miriam, don't worry about it! You're a student, we have full-time jobs."

Miriam's purple lips turned downward briefly, giving Kaity the impression that she didn't like accepting anything she considered charity. "Okay, but just until I graduate."

"Deal!" Anabelle said. "All right, ladies, a hot bath is calling my name. See you on Wednesday night, yeah?"

They all waved goodbye and scattered to their cars, and Kaity finally checked her texts.

Gabe had written: *Happy to be your arm candy for your work shindig, remind me of the date? Also, still interested in shooting?*

Kaity breathed a sigh of relief. She hadn't made things irreparably weird the previous night (not that she cared, she reminded herself), and it looked like she was still on track to give every appearance that she'd moved on from her marriage at her work function. A few weeks ago, she wasn't sure why anyone would want to photograph her, but now, she felt pumped up from pole class and dinner: Miriam and Anabelle thought she was interesting, and she was learning new things that her body could do, every time she set foot in the studio.

The way John had approached pole-dancing—as a marital aid—had been cringeworthy. But Kaity found herself wondering if maybe there was, if one approached it obliquely, some merit to the idea. Looking back, her marriage wasn't great, and maybe it wasn't worth saving. But she'd spent a lot of her life unhappy with who she was, and if this alchemical combination of exercise and art and sensuality helped make her enjoy herself more, well, perhaps she should stick with it.

She lifted her phone, and texted Gabe: *Yes. Just say when*. And she left it at that, and drove home, enjoying the glow of her newfound friends and confidence.

Kaity's text arrived while Gabe was catching up with Alex over a beer.

"Okay, so, can you weigh in on this?" Gabe asked Alex.

Alex rolled her eyes and hoisted her beer, a local kolsch.

"Oh god, did you fuck it up with Kaity? She seemed like she's got her shit together, so it must have been you who messed up."

"Hey, hey," Gabe protested. "I don't think I messed up. You met her, she's a little guarded, and I guess she's still getting over her divorce or whatever."

"Or whatever?" Alex parroted back mockingly. "Dude, I thought I taught you better than that. If you want to get in her pants, or better yet, get in her pants and get invited for a repeat, you need to empathize with where she's coming from. Don't 'whatever' your way out of actually connecting with her emotionally, even if it just ends up being a fling." Rant over, she took a triumphant sip of beer.

Gabe ran a hand through his hair. He should have been editing wedding photos right now, so getting chewed out was especially not his idea of fun. Still...Alex was his best friend for a reason. She knew him inside and out, and so if she had advice tailored to his situation, he should listen to it.

"Fine," he said, managing to sound only a little huffy. "Tell me, O Wise One, the time-proven secrets of understanding women so that I may better seduce them without ruining anything in the process."

Alex smirked. Today she was still in her work clothes, the jeans and T-shirt she'd worn under her coveralls to work in the warehouse. Gabe had heard all about the still-sexist beliefs of people in those jobs from Alex, but since Mariontown was such a hub for shipping, anyone who could handle heavy machinery was paid well and kept on, so long as they could handle any harassment that came their way. Alex could handle herself; Gabe knew that much.

"Okay, so first question, are you into her?"

Gabe frowned, and took a pause to sip on his coffee porter (he doubted the caffeine levels were high enough to impact him, but he anticipated another late night doing photo editing).

"I don't know, actually. I'm not looking for anything long-term, and we had this whole agreement, mostly to spite the other people in our lives. She's cute, and she's smart, and unlike some of the artsy women I've dated, she's definitely got her shit together." He recalled one crystal-selling lady who had emphatically not had her shit together.

"That was not really an answer," Alex observed.

"Dude, you know me too well," Gabe said, and took another sip of beer. "I...kind of like her? Could start to like her? I would definitely take her to bed. I dunno, I just get the sense that we're looking for different things and she's sorta fragile and I don't really want to get tangled up in all that."

"Okay, I can work with that," Alex said. "Here's my take," and leaned back in her stool, crossing muscled arms across her chest. "You kinda like her. And she kinda likes you, based on what you said after the whole two-attempts-at-massage thing. You have this agreement, though, that keeps things casual and firmly in the realm of just-friends. I think if you want to sleep with her, you'll have to make a bid to end the agreement and date for real. It doesn't have to be, like, totally committed, but I dunno, man, if her marriage ended in him cheating on her or something like that, you're gonna have a hard sell asking to be not exclusive while you're just dating casually. But honestly, it might be worth a shot to explore with her and see if there's something real there."

Gabe made a moue of distaste.

"Oh, come on," Alex retorted. "When was the last time you dated anyone who was remotely relationship-material? High school?"

"No,'" Gabe replied, "I was too fucked up about my mom's death to be dating anyone back then." He went for another sip of beer, appalled at his own honesty, since he didn't like talking or thinking about that time.

Alex rolled her eyes. "I'm sorry, man, I didn't mean to bring that up. But also, are you going to use that excuse for never getting close to anyone for your whole life?"

Gabe's veins froze. He stood up. "Hey, it's been fun," he ground out in Alex's direction. He downed the rest of his beer and signaled to the bartender that he was ready to pay.

Alex hunched over her beer and got out her phone. "You know that's why we're friends, Gabe. I won't bullshit you because I've known you too long."

Gabe dug out his debit card and paid. "I know, Alex. Doesn't mean you're not an asshole sometimes."

She smirked. "I know. Love you too. Text me sometime, yeah? I wanna hear how this saga goes."

"Get a life," Gabe called over his shoulder as he walked out of the bar.

Alex raised her glass in salute and muttered, "You too, man. You too."

Chapter 17

In the second half of the slinky choreo class, Kaity began to sweat as Sophia outlined what the choreography would actually look like.

It's only two minutes, she reminded herself. I can do anything for two minutes. Hell, Anabelle had once dragged her to a hot yoga class that went for an hour and fifteen minutes, and Kaity had been so drenched with sweat after that she'd struggled to peel off her sports bra.

The first half of the class had focused on refining their crawls, followed by working on proper positioning for bridges (thankfully not the full kind with the hands involved; their shoulders were the weight-bearing body parts here). They practiced gyrating their hips while in the bridge, and Kaity felt silly pumping her hips and up and down, by herself on her back in a dance studio. Even worse, her period had arrived that morning, so she felt bloated and a little gross. She'd gone with baggy sweats and a bat-wing sweater to hide her bloating, so she felt the opposite of sexy based on her attire as well.

What was the point of learning to use her hips anyway, if she never really enjoyed the process? Either she felt too fat to be worthy of wearing cute clothes and fully inhabiting her body, or if she thought maybe she'd want to be with someone (like Gabe), she spooked herself and ended up alone anyway.

Kaity's motions must have become increasingly distressed, because Sophia knelt by her side. "Hey, you doing okay?"

Plopping her butt down on the dance floor, Kaity started to talk but felt a hitch in her breath. Oh my god, do not cry, she thought to herself.

She pressed her lips together and shook her head. Sophia stayed kneeling by her side for a moment before sitting down to face her.

"I know learning a lot of new stuff can be overwhelming," Sophia said. "You're doing great, even if it doesn't feel like it."

The petty voice inside Kaity's head, which she'd worked so hard to keep cooped up at work, around Georgia, came spilling out.

"But you're a natural at this stuff! And everything you do looks good on your body, with your curves! Me, I'm just—" Kaity bit off the words, already regretting talking.

"Look at me," Sophia said in a commanding yet gentle voice. Kaity raised her eyes to Sophia's, seeing that they were a blue-gray behind her glasses. Her face was pretty, with a dusting of freckles, and her countenance held none of the witchy red-haired vixen who'd done all of the fancy splitty things at the showcase.

"I've been studying this slinky style of pole for five years, and I was a pole dancer for three years before that. When I first started learning, I felt really awkward too. And I couldn't talk to anyone about it, since I'm a teacher. Middle school," she added, smiling wryly.

"Sophia's just my stage name. I had to work at the moves to get them to feel natural, and one of the first steps was not comparing myself to others. I wasn't the fastest or best student in my certification class. I had to work for everything you see as coming naturally now."

Kaity tried to process this information. She knew she had a habit of being too hard on herself, and she suspected she was being gently called out on it.

Sophia continued, still wearing her soft smile, "Sometimes this really embodied form of dance can bring stuff up for people: painful experiences, trauma, and so on. And that's normal, in a way—whatever you feel, however you experience your body, is valid. But I will say this: if you slow down and enjoy the movements for what they are, you'll get more out of it. You'll maybe process some stuff. But if you dig deep, you'll find a reason to come back to the dance studio, again and again, and it'll give back as much as you give it."

She stood, and announced, "All right everyone, new drill!" When she had the attention of everyone in the room, she said, "We're going to keep working on our bridges and hip circles in them, but in a different way. I wasn't going to give us this prompt for another few weeks, but I think it'll benefit us now. I'm going to put on a song, and call out prompts during it. You'll stay in a bridge the whole time, except for when you need to come down to your back and rest. Then, you can practice the side-to-side roll we did earlier, and when you're on your back again, you can resume. Got it?"

Kaity nodded along with the rest, and silently hoped that she wasn't about to be the cause of massive resentment due to a difficult drill dropping on all of them early.

Sophia put a new song on; this one was slow, languid, taking its time dropping the beat.

Kaity eased down onto her back again and got ready to push up into a bridge.

"All right, when you start doing your hip circles, try to go to your fullest range of motion without overextending yourself," Sophia said over the music.

Kaity pushed up into her bridge, then paused and took stock. What was her fullest range of motion? How would she know? She pushed her hips towards the ceiling, then slowly starting dropping them to the right. She let her butt graze the ground before taking her hips to the left, and up above again. Then she reversed the circle.

It felt...good? Almost like the kind of stretch she might take in bed, on one of her rare lazy mornings?

Sophia's voice interrupted her thoughts, "Take that pace, and slow it down."

Kaity did another round of hip circles in her bridge, aware of every inch that her hips moved through space. She went twice in the same direction, then once in the other direction before setting her hips on the ground. She extended her arms above, and let her hips move first, rolling her onto one side and then onto her belly. She tried to keep the pace slow. Again, she let her hips lead the next movement, taking her onto her back again.

As she was pushing up into another bridge, Sophia spoke again, "Now, think about your hands. Where are they? Are they touching your floor, or the body? Can you change their location?"

Kaity noticed that both hands were pressed palms-down, flat to the floor. She left one hand down to brace—moving to her fullest range of motion meant almost pulling herself off balance—and brought the other up. She bent her elbow to fold her hand into her chest, and left her fingertips laying on her collarbone. What now?

"One thing you can think about," Sophia continued, "is touching yourself in a way that feels good to you. Don't worry about how it looks, focus on how it *feels*."

Kaity let her fingertips trail along the line of her collarbone. The light touch felt good. She took a long inhale. The music had become quiet for a few moments and then the beat picked back up, so she started moving her hips again, slowly, deliberately, focusing on what felt good. Her right hand migrated up her neck, to gently trail along her face, and then down, down her sides, down her belly, and for once she didn't care that her shirt had lifted to show some skin, she just played with the hem while continuing to circle her hips in the bridge.

The song ended, and Kaity let her hips come to the ground, then rolled to one side and sat up.

Along with everyone else, she looked to Sophia for instructions on what was next. But she also glanced at everyone else's faces briefly, and saw that she wasn't the only one who seemed to be coming out of a trance. The whole room was quiet, contemplative.

"That was beautiful," Sophia murmured. "You all looked caught up in the moment, like you took a moment for yourselves. The amazing thing is that when we do this in our dancing, no matter how we might think we look, we end up having an inner experience that translates into outward appearance. And that's what we'll work on capturing in our choreography, even though it'll all be planned out in advance."

With that, the class shifted to the choreo planning, and the dreaded topic of costuming had come up.

"So, this is a sexy choreography, and I want everyone to feel comfortable with what they're wearing, but also to match somewhat," Sophia said. "I also don't want anyone to have to spend a ton of money, so we'll pick something simple as our unifying theme. The only thing I'll require is black kneepads. Sound good?"

The three more advanced dancers—Nina, April, and Mo—had taken the lead in the conversation, talking about garter-strap shorts and peek-a-boo bras and other mystical items. Then they seemed to realize that there were newbies in the room and consulted Anabelle, Kaity, and Miriam.

"I vote shorts," Nina said. "We could pick a color and everyone could buy shorts in that color?"

"I'm good with shorts," Anabelle said, and everyone else nodded.

"Shorts with fishnets?" Miriam suggested.

Sophia interjected, "That's a cool look, and appropriate to the dance we'll be doing, but please keep in mind that you'll need to practice in them before performing in them, and they'll probably snag, so you'll need to buy multiple pairs."

Everyone agreed that it wasn't a problem, and so they settled on black shorts, black fishnets underneath, and a black top of one's choosing.

"Can it be a whole shirt or does it have to be a sports bra or crop top?" Kaity asked.

This spurred a new round of considerations, leading Sophia to once again weigh in. "Given the choreo, since we are spending a lot of time on the ground, it should be a top that doesn't roll up or scrunch. So a sports bra would be ideal, but if you want more coverage, maybe you could find a bodysuit, sheer or opaque."

"Shopping!" Anabelle mouthed at Kaity.

Kaity nodded, then tapped her wrist and shrugged to indicate that she wasn't sure when. She probably needed to get her own kneepads anyway, rather than continuing to sweat into Anabelle's.

The remainder of the evening was devoted to starting to piece together moves for the final choreography, and learning the sequence demanded enough of Kaity's attention span that she completely forgot that she'd made tentative plans with Gabe until after she'd exited the studio, feeling tired but accomplished and oddly peaceful. The mild cramps had subsided, and with that excuse evaporating, she decided that she felt good and ready to tackle step one of a photoshoot.

Chapter 18

A fter one or two false starts, Gabe was determined to actually photograph this time. The next Snap-dragon showcase wasn't for another month or more, and he itched to do something creative. Alex's words still stung, implying that he didn't have much of a life be-cause he hadn't let anyone in since his mom and brother had died. But he'd taken steps to let Kaity in, and he would definitely be making plans to shoot with other dancers. Every wedding season threatened to crush his soul, and every year, he found something to give him life.

If nothing else, he assumed Kaity would need to ease in, and they'd fiddle with some concepts, take some preliminary shots, and then call it a night.

He assumed wrong.

When she poked her head inside the studio door and then let herself in, her first few motions were deliberate and assertive. None of her usual hesitation showed in her body...which made Gabe hesitate in his approach. Something had changed, but he didn't know what and didn't know how to ask.

Instead he settled for, "How was your day?"

She smiled. "Not bad, actually. This new dance class I'm taking is ramping up, but in a good way. How about you?"

"Same old. Wedding season is ramping up, which means almost more work than I can handle. So it's a good thing, but a busy thing."

"Well then, let's get right to it," Kaity said, setting her purse down. "Do you have a costume I can change into?"

Gabe pointed to the screen, where a few different drape-y robes hung over the edge. "Take your pick," he said.

Kaity disappeared behind the screen, leaving Gabe to stew over the intangible differences he was noticing. Maybe she'd had an especially good day at work? Though that seemed unlikely based on what she'd told him about the annoying ex-sister-in-law. He made a mental note to ask Alex, if Alex was done being a jerk, about unanticipated reasons why women might be extra confident.

Within minutes, Kaity had emerged in a robe—was it a chiton or peplos? he'd learned the difference in art history but forgotten—that stole his breath.

The robe was a warm peachy color, and on its own was fairly formless, since it was one of those garments meant to fit a range of body sizes and shapes. These sorts of items were an artist's best friend, since one purchase could look good on a variety of models.

Kaity had, judging by the lack of visible bra straps, donned the robe over nothing but underwear, and used one of the plain cords also hanging over the folding screen to gather the robe's folds at her waist. The wide cut of the collar exposed her collarbones, and the loose armholes of the sleeveless robe exposed a faint bruise on the inside of one shoulder. Gabe couldn't help but notice how the corded belt highlighted the narrow spot in her waist between her breasts and her hips, the curves of which attracted his eye more than he'd care to admit to himself.

Her brown, faintly-wavy hair cascaded down to her mid-back, and her hazel eyes were, for once, open and unguarded.

"How do I look?" she asked.

"Like a goddess," Gabe answered with a smile, his flirtatious instincts kicking back in.

She blushed, and dipped her chin. But it came right back up before too long, and Kaity walked over to the canvas backdrop at one wall. It hung from the ceiling, and spilled out onto the floor, extended a few yards from the wall.

"Can I sit on the floor?" Kaity asked.

"Yes, of course," he replied.

She sank to the floor, one knee bent and the other leg crossed over it. Even swimming in the folds of fabric, her curves shone through, in a way Gabe found both aesthetically appealing and arousing. She let one hand brush the floor to her side, and rest the fingertips of the other on her collarbone.

Gabe paused with a critical eye, and grabbed his camera, also flicking some buttons on the standing umbrella reflector to adjust the settings of the lighting. He snapped a few pictures, looked at them, adjusted the lighting once more, and then looked back at Kaity.

"That's perfect, stay there if you can," he said, and then he was working.

He knelt to change the angle, and saw her lips part slightly, as though she were lost in reverie. He noticed her fingertips lightly caressing my collarbone, and her eyes closed dreamily.

"All right, feel free to take a break or find a new pose," he directed her. He sat back on his heels to examine some of the photos, and while they'd need some touching up—they always did—there were at least a handful of really good ones. Kaity looked, of all things, vulnerable. And it looked good on her. For some reason, seeing her let her guard down around him warmed his chest.

When he looked back at her, she'd settled into a position, reclining on her back but with her hips twisted, as though she was about to roll onto her side. This spared him having to explain what *contrapposto* was and why it made everyone look better.

"You are intuitively doing a very good job of this," he said to Kaity, after she'd moved through a few more poses.

She smiled dreamily. "My dance teacher said something today that just kinda stuck with me, that I should focus on how I feel instead of how I look. So I'm just doing things that feel good, that feel authentic, and hoping it translates."

He chuckled. "It certainly does. I think we have enough for now to establish some concepts and future directions. Shall we call it?"

"Sure. I'll go change back." And she stood smoothly, leaving Gabe to continue to wonder what had changed. Like, she'd said something about dance class, but surely there was more to it than that? If not, he'd been missing out by not working with more dancers this whole time.

Gabe had taken a seat in one of the comfy armchairs by the time she emerged, back in sweats and the super loose sweater she'd entered in. Even so, she looked radiant.

"Do you want to hang out some more?" he asked. "We could grab a drink, or I could give you a massage?"

Kaity smiled at him, and the smile was both beautiful and self-contained in a way he couldn't entirely describe, as though she'd found the secret to happiness and was keeping it to herself. Maybe it was wistful? Or maybe that's how he felt in response.

"Thanks, but I'm heading home for tea and some time on my couch," she said. "This was fun...let me know how the pics turn out?"

Gabe donned a winning smile as he showed her out. Go figure, he'd finally determined that he actually was kinda into her, and she seemed to not return the sentiment. Maybe he needed a more elaborate plan to seduce her. He bid her farewell, and then, fighting the habitual impulse to skip out to a bar or brewery, sat down to transfer the photos to his laptop so he could start editing them. He realized after she'd left that they hadn't actually pinned down a story or a theme, but maybe a theme would suggest itself.

A dozen photos in, he realized that the theme was one of awakening. And while Kaity clearly hadn't been intending to look seductive in any of the pictures, he found his desire for her growing, and he was entirely unsure what to do with this knowledge, having already been rebuffed once.

With a sigh, he picked up his phone to text Alex. With any luck, her advice would be spot on, as it often was.

Which Gabe needed, since he at least had to sort his feelings out enough to hold up his end of the bargain and be Kaity's date to her work function.

Kaity floated in through her front door. She wasn't sure how one dance class out of half a dozen had turned out to be better than therapy, but it was. Hoping it wasn't too late to draw a bath and still get enough sleep for the next work day, she paused to rifle through the stack of mail she'd brought in earlier.

Most were routine bills and advertisements. One letter stuck out.

It was a letter from her ex-husband's attorney.

Chapter 19

Kaity put on her most professional outfit to go into work the next day, and marched into Georgia's office.

"What is this?" she demanded, slapping the letter down on the desk.

Georgia turned blue eyes on Kaity, a look of annoyance on her face. "What is what?"

"This," Kaity thrust the letter towards Georgia. "Your brother thinks I lied in the court deposition about my income. Now why would he think that?"

Georgia rolled her eyes. Today's lipstick was a cherry red, and her nails were immaculate golden moons. "Calm down. I told him what my salary was, and he must've calculated yours in relation to it and figured it was higher than you'd let on."

Kaity shook with silent rage. "I shared a bank account with that man for five years, he knew what my damn salary was."

Shrugging, Georgia turned back to her computer. "Then you have nothing to worry about."

Kaity snatched up the letter and stalked out of the office. Anabelle was the legal expert for the divorced ladyfriends; she would know what to do. Once Kaity was done with work and could show her the letter, anyway.

A canceled lunch meeting allowed Kaity to escape from the office and rendezvous with Anabelle in Irlington again, this time at a cider place that served food. Kaity ordered a tart cherry cider alongside her smoked turkey sandwich, deeming it a good day for a lunchtime drink.

"It's basically bogus," Anabelle concluded after looking at the letter and hearing Kaity's account of the divorce. "Indiana is a fifty-fifty state, and this is where you got divorced, so since you split everything, you're in the clear."

Kaity had vented for a good twenty minutes about the divorce proceedings, the agonizing tallying of their possessions and accounts. But since she and John had each owned their own cars and had paid off their student loans and were just renting a house—they'd only recently moved to Mariontown from Louisville, and were deciding which neighborhood they wanted to live in prior to purchasing a house—they didn't have any debts to split, just assets. Though John's salary was slightly higher than hers, her job offered better benefits, and thus their 401ks were roughly equivalent. It had seemed easy at the time: verbally agree on how to split up shared possessions, divide their checking account in half, and part ways.

"So why the hell did I get this letter?" Kaity brusquely asked.

Anabelle sighed. "You're not the first one in our group to face this issue. I could pull up the stats, and they're horrifying, but a lot of domestic violence occurs after the woman has left a bad marriage. It's just a bid for control, an attempt to unsettle you, to maybe scare you enough to make you come back."

Kaity stared at her friend. Anabelle had never spoken much about her own divorce, instead seeming to dwell in the present moment, surrounded by smiles and sparkles. Kaity began to wonder how much darkness had accrued under the surface, and when it might be the right time to ask about it.

"Do I need to lawyer up?" Kaity asked finally.

"I'm not a lawyer," Anabelle said for the fifth time in the conversation, "but probably not. Your paperwork should speak for itself. You keep such meticulous records anyway."

Kaity glumly chewed on her sandwich, washing it down with sips of cider. Here she was, finally enjoying single life a little bit, and her ex had to come rain on her parade.

"Hey," Anabelle said, reaching a hand across the table to put on Kaity's shoulder. "It's gonna be okay. It might not feel like it, but it is." Kaity managed a wan smile in response.

"Thank you. It just feels like everything sucks right now."

"How are things with Gabe?"

"Oh, I don't know. For a while I thought I might hook up with him, but I think we're better as friends. I don't want to fall into bed with the first guy to show interest in me after my divorce, you know? But we had a fun photoshoot last night, and I felt really sensual and into myself after choreo class, and I'm excited to see the pictures."

"Ooh, I can't wait to see those too, I bet you look amazing," Anabelle gushed. "I wonder if he'll be photographing the next showcase, too."

Kaity groaned, put down her sandwich, and put her head down on the backs of her hands. "I'd totally forgotten about that. So I guess I need to make sure things don't get awkward between us once our little ruse is done."

"Don't forget, we need to go shopping before then too! Remember, Sofia said it's essential to practice in anything we wear before we perform in it."

"Right," Kaity agreed. "Maybe this weekend, once I make some progress on this stuff with my ex?"

"I'm in," Anabelle said. "For now, though, I need to get back to work."

"I've got lunch. Thanks again for helping with this." Before leaving, Anabelle hugged Kaity and whispered in her ear, "You're going to be okay. We'll help each other through this stuff." Kaity felt warm after the hug, but she also wondered how many women Anabelle had told this to, and whether anyone had said it to Anabelle.

The end of the work day saw Kaity through half a dozen phone calls and a series of emails that confirmed what Anabelle had said: the letter was not actually anything to worry about, and the claims in it would be cleared up by sharing some paperwork.

Still, she had spent nearly 24 hours in a panicked state, which left her exhausted and a little resentful. But also, she reflected, a bit grateful to have made it out of her marriage without too much bad stuff happening until now.

As a treat, she decided to stop at the new tea shop on College Avenue.

The place was decorated a bit like someone's take-away after having read *Alice in Wonderland*, but not in at least the last decade. Overstuffed armchairs sported stripes and paisleys, while the walls were pastel with old-timey monochromatic portraits in profile on them. Cats and dodos figured prominently.

At the counter, a man around her own age greeted her and took her order. Kaity decided to splurge on the rooibos chai, and she was invited to take a seat while she waited for it. Rather than pulling out her phone to fiddle, she rolled her wrists a few times and stretched her arms above her head. It felt good to take a few breaths and try to unlock the tension of the day.

"Miss?" It was the barista (if that label applied to people who made tea as well as those who made coffee) at her side. As he put the tea—delicately foamed within its large porcelain teacup—down on the side table, he smiled at Kaity, and Kaity began to think he was a little cute. Dark brown eyes nestled in a medium-brown face, and the corners of his eyes crinkled when he smiled.

"Let me know how you like this one; I blended both the tea and the spices myself."

Kaity smiled back. "Thank you, I will." She let the tea cool for a few minutes before sipping it, and the spice blend was nicely balanced but definitely packed a punch. She texted the updates about her saga to the divorced ladyfriends group, and received a boost of alternately supportive and righteously indignant messages on her behalf. As Anabelle had implied, she wasn't the only one to have experienced this kind of manipulative grab for control, or at least intimidation, at the end of her marriage. Some of her new friends had experienced it during their marriage, a thought which made Kaity shudder.

Finally starting to unclench from stress, Kaity drank her tea, then complimented the man on her way out. He took the compliment gracefully and invited her to return anytime.

Not hard, she thought, when she didn't live far from here. Maybe Anabelle's theory of "getting out and doing things after one's divorce" was a good idea after all.

Chapter 20

The arrival of the weekend meant shopping.

Anabelle arrived at Kaity's doorstep bright and early—9am on Saturday, which was close enough—with a plan.

"All right, I'm driving, and we're getting brunch first like I texted you. You haven't eaten, have you?" No, Kaity had not eaten; she had been up late with a book and some herbal tea, which she'd purchased at the shop on College on Friday.

"Good," Anabelle announced with palpable satisfaction. They ended up at a place that served local brie melts over house-made croissants, with mimosas on one side of their table and coffee on the other. A spring salad of asparagus with shaved fennel completed the meal. As they ate, Anabelle outlined the plan: hit the mall in Nura first, since it was most likely to have stores with discounts inside, and then they could proceed to the Boutiques on Keystone as needed.

"But we're not, like, actually dancing in lingerie, right?" Kaity asked.

"I feel like that point was left ambiguous," Anabelle said, after gazing into her mimosa. "Whatever we wear has to stand up to some serious abuse given the nature of our dance, rolling around on the ground and all that. It's probably best if it's made of stretch material. And god knows it'd be nice if we could stick it in the washer on a gentle cycle instead of having to wash it in a sink or tub. But as far as what we choose at the end of the day? Black shorts, black fishnets, black tops of some sort—that leaves a lot of wiggle room."

Kaity mulled this over. She was used to only buying practical clothes, the kind that would survive multiple washings and would serve more than one purpose. Today, for instance, saw her in jean capris and a yellow blouse that had some cute gold paneling on the front; both had been purchased back in Louisville, well over a year ago. She hadn't done much shopping, especially post-divorce when finances were a little tight. Come to think of it, when was the last time she'd bought something for herself, just because she wanted to? Because it made her look especially good or feel especially good?

An hour later found Kaity close to tears in a dressing room.

"How's it going?" Anabelle called in.

"Not great," Kaity ground out. The lace bodysuit she'd tried on was cutting into her hips, leaving obvious bulges of fat that putting a pair of shorts on wouldn't disguise. The neckline didn't work, either. She couldn't say why—too wide? too low? —but it definitely didn't work with her figure.

"Will you let me come in and see?" Anabelle persisted. Kaity sighed. "Fine," she said, and opened the door to the fitting room.

"Hmm...this doesn't work on you," Anabelle agreed. "I think I saw the bodysuit in a different cut, so I'll go grab it in a size up and hand it in to you."

"Are you sure that's not too much trouble?" Kaity asked. "I just feel...ugh. Too fat to look good in this kind of thing. Plus I'm bloated, since I've got another day of my period."

"Nonsense! You just need a different style," Anabelle declared. "Try on some of these sports bras in the meantime," and she produced some hangers out of apparently nowhere.

The next bodysuit looked better, and so did the next one after that. Anabelle made the executive decision to leave these two candidates on hold while they went to the next shop on her list. Kaity was uncertain how much stamina she had left for this kind of thing; too many badly-fitting outfits on her body, in a world where high fashion was clearly intended for people way skinnier than her, had a demoralizing effect.

In between their next two stops, Kaity heard her phone ping. She pulled it out and saw that Gabe had been texting her this whole time, which she had inadvertently ignored during her dressing-room near-meltdown. She opened the texts, and stopped in her tracks.

Anabelle, already a few steps ahead of her, seemed to realize that Kaity was missing. "What is it? Are you okay?"

Kaity turned her phone screen to Anabelle, speechless.

On the screen was the first of the pics Gabe had sent from their shoot: Kaity reclining in a flowy peach gown, her brown waves spread all over her neck and shoulders, her eyes half-closed in languid pleasure. From this angle, her curves melted into the ground, rolling like gentle hilltops or mountain tops, not jutting out like she'd felt everything stuck out in the dressing room.

She looked beautiful. Peaceful. Sexy.

"Oh my god," Anabelle said. "You look fantastic!"

"I don't...I mean...that's not how I actually look, is it?"

"Yes, you do," Anabelle insisted. "I mean, the nice lighting probably helps. Gabe's a professional, he could make anyone look good. But he chose to make *you* look good. I think this is how he sees you."

Kaity rolled her eyes. "You can say that all you want, but I don't think he's into me." She also noticed that they were standing in the middle of one of the mall's walkways, and moved them to one side of the aisle, so as not to block foot traffic.

"That's because you haven't let him be into you," Anabelle replied. "You're doing each other a favor by showing up as dates to your respective events, but I don't think you're giving him a chance. He's a catch. I think even if he made a pass at you, you wouldn't register it, because you're so deep into the story of your own—"

"My own what?" Kaity asked, narrowing her eyes.

"Look," Anabelle said, raising her hands defensively. "I'm just talking from experience. But right after my divorce, I felt damaged. I felt unlovable. If some cute guy had thrown himself at me, I probably wouldn't have even noticed. Like, I might've noticed enough for a quick rebound, but that would've been it."

For once, Kaity spoke without measuring her words. "Anabelle, we're different people. Your divorce sucked, my divorce sucked. I'm not ready to date yet, and the fact that Gabe and I are just friends and accomplices is not up for discussion. I don't think he's hitting on me with these pictures...if anything, I get the impression that he doesn't tend to date women he shoots because he'd rather keep things professional and not open the door to any rumors."

"Kaity, I'm sorry...obviously you can do whatever you want, or not do anything, since it's your life. I just thought...ugh, nevermind." Anabelle started walking again.

Dazed, Kaity tried to figure out what had just happened.

"No, I'm sorry, wait up," Kaity said, scurrying forward. She caught up with Anabelle, still feeling her heart in her throat. "I know you're not trying to be all prescriptive. You're a great friend. It's just...every time I think about caring about someone enough again to be hurt by them, it makes me feel sick to my stomach."

"I get it," Anabelle said after a short pause. "We all have our post-divorce damage. I'll try to not comment on yours if you try not to comment on mine."

"I wasn't even aware you still had post-divorce damage," Kaity said. "It's been, what, three years since yours?"

"Yeah," Anabelle said. "But you don't see me dating much, do you? I've still got some issues."

Kaity impulsively hugged her friend. "Let's finish our shopping trip," she suggested.

"All right," Anabelle said. "But you have to show me the rest of those pics from Gabe! I promise I'll stop implying things about the way he sees you, and I'll just praise you for how hot you look in them."

Kaity chuckled. "All right. Let's do this." There were only a few more pictures to scroll through, but Kaity looked pretty damn good in all of them, and she found herself wondering if she should, indeed, be treating these as a purely platonic gift from Gabe.

"Are you kinda dancing in these?" Anabelle asked. "Some of these poses look like movements we pass through in slinky choreo class."

"Yeah, you caught me, I have no clue how to model but I figured I might as well try applying the ideas Sophia had explained in class, how in dance it's less about how we look than how we feel, and if we're feeling ourselves in the moment, we might just end up looking good too."

"Makes sense to me," Anabelle said. "I'm just so happy you seemed to have a good time, and you got some nice photos out of it. And hopefully a confidence boost..." and she winked lasciviously, "...since we still need to hit three more stores!"

Sighing, Kaity put away her phone. "Well, I did block off all day for this. Let's go find some sexy apparel." In the back of her mind, though, she started wondering how much she really needed it, since Gabe could make her look good in a heap of fabric. So maybe she wasn't as much of a cow as her ex-husband had insisted, and maybe she shouldn't have spent so much time seeking the approval of someone who wouldn't have been satisfied with her no matter how she looked or what she did.

This line of thought was mercifully cut short with an array of frilly things for her to consider trying on, and Kaity did her best to just go with it.

Chapter 21

Somehow it was already week 6 of the beginning pole class, and they were gearing up to try a pole sit after a climb or two. Jenny gave them a bit of extra time after warm-up to stretch anything else that needed stretching, recommending some additional shoulder and hamstring stretches.

So Kaity asked Miriam how classes were going (not good, was the answer, as finals drew near; Kaity offered to help with anything tech-related) and then asked Anabelle how her new sports bra was working out (it being one of the results of their shopping trip; it was black, hence suitable for the choreo performance, but Anabelle had been worried that the peek-a-boo cut-out beneath her breasts but above the band of the sports bra might prove troublesome). So far, nothing had popped out that shouldn't have.

Then, after running their existing spins and moves, Jenny began to instruct them on a straight-legged pole sit. She effortlessly climbed up the pole, held on with her hands, extended both legs parallel to the floor, and miraculously stayed put with only one hand lightly on the pole.

From up there, Jenny told them: "The secret to a pole sit is actually in the hips. If you look closely, you'll see that I have tilted my hips to the left, so the pole is almost touching the top of my right thigh. If I try to keep my hips square to the pole, here's what happens." She put both hands firmly back on the pole just in time to catch herself from sliding down.

"Now, when I tilt my hips again, watch what happens." She emphatically rolled her hips to the left, catching the pole securely once more. "You'll also notice that I'm crossing my top foot—in this case my right foot—on top of the left, and hooking my ankles." Jenny then rolled her hips the other direction, so her left hip was lifted, and demonstrated crossing her feet the other way, with the left foot hooked on top of the right.

Kaity swallowed, feeling her pulse pick up. This looked like it'd result in lots of burning sensations on her thighs, since there was a lot of real estate there.

"One other important tip: you need the pole to be close to your crotch, not so far down your thighs it's almost to your knees. That would make it extremely difficult to get a good grip." She scooted her hips away from the pole a little bit, wobbling to show that she was now unstable.

"All right, so let's all give this a try! You can start from the ground and do a pull-up on the pole to wrap your legs around, and try the straight-legged sit from there." With that, Jenny hopped down from the pole and stood expectantly.

Everyone managed some rendition of the move. Kaity tried to tell herself that it wasn't terribly scary, only being a few feet up from the ground. Her inner thighs started to burn as expected after just one repetition, so she wasn't sure how many more she had in her.

"Looking good! Give it a climb or two, and I can come around to spot as needed."

Kaity wiped down her pole, and also swiped the cloth around her thighs after observing others doing it. She decided to watch the first few attempts by others; she wasn't necessarily afraid of heights, but she didn't relish the thought of being too far from the ground, in an out-of-the-ordinary position, without much to hold her up there. Her arms were slowly getting stronger, but something like a straight pull-up was probably well outside her reach still. Then again, she'd always carried a lot of weight in her thighs, so maybe this move would help leverage that?

Lin was the first one up the pole, and she crossed her ankles in a perfect imitation of Jenny, then took one hand off the pole, staying in that pose for a few moments. Jenny was hovering nearby, and she clapped. "Great job! Who's next?"

Anabelle and Miriam climbed next, and after a little fiddling, each one nailed it. Kaity took that to mean it was her turn.

She put both hands on the pole a little higher than face height, got one foot onto the back of the pole, and lifted her whole body up to wrap her other foot around the front of the pole. So far, so good. Once her knees were gripping the pole and holding her in place, she moved her hands up a few inches, then clung to the pole with all her arm strength so she could move her feet up too.

Figuring that two climbs would be enough, Kaity held onto the pole with her hands while straightening her legs so her toes now pointed straight out. She kept both hands on the pole, made sure her hips had a strong tilt to them, and crossed her top ankle over.

She took one hand off the pole, and posed, feeling like a rockstar for a moment.

Then the burning in her thighs caught up with her. The skin was being pulled in various directions, and she could no longer ignore the fiery sensation.

Kaity hopped down from the pole, and tried to shake it off.

"Owww," she said. She glanced down, and saw red marks forming, not extensive enough to be considered welts, but still.

"Right there with you," Anabelle replied.

"You all got this right away!" Jenny crowed. "Now, try it again, and cross the other ankle on top while leaning the other direction. Most people end up preferring one side over the other, but it's important to work both sides."

Kaity shook out her legs and arms, wiped down the pole, and determined to give it another try. Last time she'd crossed her right ankle over her left, and tilted her right hips up, so this time she'd try it the other way around.

She managed two climbs up the pole, grasped it with both hands, and straightened her legs. She tried to point her toes the whole time, while crossing her left foot over her right, and making sure her ankles were locked. Left hip lifted, she felt a familiar burn in the skin of her inner thighs. It was as though her skin was *tugging* and there was plenty of excess skin to be tugged around, and Kaity lost herself in shame for one moment, clinging to the pole.

But the movement seemed fairly locked in. So Kaity took one hand off the pole and arched her back, wishing for once that she'd set up her phone to capture the moment, as some of the women in her class did whenever the opportunity presented itself.

"Looking good, Kaity!" came Anabelle's enthusiastic shout from below. Kaity twisted herself around by leaning into her thighs even more, so she could see herself in the mirror. She did, indeed, look good. She leaned in to switch her hands, and—

—something came loose, and she was falling.

Chapter 22

K aity landed with a thump.

She felt her flesh slam onto the floor, and boy, there must have been a lot of flesh to slam, because the noise was so loud she felt herself cringe.

It took willpower to not retreat into her worst judgments: that she was too fat for this, too fat to be attractive, too insecure as well. Her face flamed with embarrassment before she made herself analyze the situation and scan herself for injuries.

She wasn't entirely sure, but she must've loosened her feet, or ankles, or thighs, or all of the above while on the pole.

"Are you okay?" Jenny was immediately at her side.

Dazed, Kaity looked at Jenny, and then back at the pole. She nodded, then resumed taking a brief inventory of her body.

"I think...I just fell on my butt?" she offered, her voice a shamed whisper.

Jenny offered her a hand up. "That's what it looked like. Did you accidentally let go of the pole?"

Kaity, now standing, reached a hand down to pat her butt. It was a little achy from the impact. "I think so."

"Well, take a minute, and get your bearings. And rest more if you need it. Sometimes this kind of thing happens, where we loosen crucial muscles without realizing it. In the future, we have a better sense of which muscles we need to engage in order to stay on the pole."

Kaity went to refill her water bottle, and Anabelle rushed over. "Kaity! Are you okay?"

"Yeah, I think so. Might be a little sore tomorrow, though," and Kaity gingerly poked her butt with her free hand.

Anabelle gave her a quick hug. "No more falling, okay?!"

"Not on purpose, I swear," Kaity replied.

She took it easy for the rest of class, trying to be extra mindful every time she walked around the pole or stepped into a spin. Nothing seemed to be really wrong with her, so clearly she hadn't injured herself, but she still felt spooked.

"Hey, I don't know if I'm hungry tonight," she told Anabelle after class. "Grab dinner next week?" Her apologetic excuses were accepted, and then she was driving home, fantasizing about a hot bath. Miriam had vanished after class had let out, and Kaity felt a bit miffed about her new friend not asking if she was okay.

Unlocking the door to her apartment, Kaity suddenly felt pathetic coming home alone, to an empty space. The fact that she'd found her feet so fast after her divorce was a badge of pride; this apartment was an achievement. Even if it felt lonely sometimes.

Kaity assembled a salad out of things in her fridge, topping it with two chopped hard-boiled eggs.

While eating, she fiddled with her phone. She thought about texting Gabe, and finally justified it to herself by considering that she could've died today on the pole. Well, it wasn't likely, not at that height, and her head wasn't going to be the first thing to hit the floor unless she was seriously screwing up. Even so.

She set her fork down, picked it up, and set it down again. The ghost of an embarrassed flush floated over her face again, as she anticipated rejection. Then she wrote: *Rough night at pole, almost died, am hurting. What are you up to?*

He texted back faster than she'd anticipated: *Want me to come over? massage/talking?*

Relieved, Kaity wrote back: *Yes*, followed by her address.

She made two cups of tea and had them set on the coffee table when Gabe knocked. She gingerly walked to the door and let him in.

His eyebrows knit together and he paused in her door frame.

"Are you okay, Kaity?"

She walked, almost hobbled, back to her seat. "People keep asking me that. Yes. I took a fall. I'm fine." She heard her speech being clipped, hoped she didn't sound too emotional.

Gabe followed her over, and found his own seat. "Well, what can I do to help? Would a massage be good, or would it just irritate where you fell further?" He spotted the mug of tea meant for him, picked it up, cradled it in his hands. "Wait, where did you fall? Do I need to avoid touching you in certain places?"

Kaity's cheeks burned in a blush. "I was climbing the pole, and trying out a new style of sit. I fell on my butt. Luckily it's got a lot of padding, I guess."

Gabe smiled at her over the rim of his mug. "Well, I'm glad you're okay."

"I don't know if I'm okay!" she cried out, in an uncharacteristic outburst. "God, this sounds dumb, but it made me realize how vulnerable I am, and how lonely." She felt her cheeks continue to burn, and the skin on her inner thighs, too.

Gabe set his mug down, very slowly. "Kaity, what are you—?"

She didn't wait for him to answer. She didn't feel like she could wait any longer. She launched herself from her seat into his arms, into his lap, and found his lips, and was finally kissing him.

Gabe could tell that something was off about Katie's tone when she had texted him, and moreso when she had let him into her apartment. In the month or so they'd known each other, she'd always come across as controlled and guarded. Whatever had happened to her tonight had shaken her.

When she started kissing him, Gabe was not expecting it. He had sharply inhaled the scent of her, half lost in the kiss and half analyzing what the hell was happening. He'd practically been throwing himself at her the prior time they'd hung out, and she'd breezed out of his studio as if he hadn't existed. Even Alex hadn't known what to say about that incident, counseling patience.

So Gabe had resigned himself to the possibility that Kaity was not terribly interested in him, that she was better as a friend, that they'd be artistic collaborators if nothing else. Even tonight, just in a loose-fitting T-shirt and joggers, with her wavy brown hair down around her shoulders, she looked cute and cozy, such that he wanted to touch her to see if she felt as soft as she looked.

Now, with her in his lap, he was free to do exactly that.

Kaity's lips were soft, and her breath smelled faintly of herbal tea. She had started out by kissing him hungrily, nipping at his own lips until he'd opened them to let her in, to let her explore a bit with her tongue, and then pull back to allow him to do the same.

While they kissed, Gabe lifted his hands, which had settled on her hips, to trail them up her sides. He felt that under the soft T-shirt she had on, there was no bra. He decided to steer clear of sensitive areas until it was clear that she really wanted him, so he brought his hands around to her shoulders and back, caressing them.

From where she straddled him, he could feel her hips start to work, subtly but rhythmically. Then she stopped kissing him in order to pull off her shirt. Well, that was a pretty clear signal to progress.

Gabe stayed where he was, leaning back a bit, in order to take in the sight of her. Her skin was smooth, creamy, gorgeous. Her breasts looked lovely, tinged with a flush that was also creeping up her neck. He decided telling her how she looked was a good idea.

"You're beautiful," he murmured, and pulled her in closer to kiss again. He felt her smile against his lips, and felt her fingers interlace in his hair at the nape of his neck. As she leaned over him, he felt her breasts pressing against his chest, turning him on further. Finally, he gave in to temptation and began to gently cup her breasts with each hand; they fit nicely into his palms. Based on Kaity's moans, he went from gently cupping to gently squeezing, while her hips ground even more against him.

As they made out, Gabe found himself entranced with how she moved. He'd slept with dancers before, but there was something authentic about how Kaity moved, as though once she'd stopped constantly monitoring herself, she was just being herself with him, inhabiting her body and letting it respond to every kiss and caress.

And he felt himself responding too, shifting to accommodate his suddenly-tight pants.

He pulled away to lower his lips to the top of one breast, then the other. Looking up, he saw her eyes close and her mouth part with pleasure. She took a shuddering inhale, and Gabe resumed giving her breasts attention. He was gratified to feel her hips shifting into his faster. He switched his mouth over to her other breast, playing with the nipple with his tongue, and used his free hand to slide down the front of her pants.

Hot wetness greeted him, and Gabe felt his arousal surge in response. God, but he wanted her.

He freed up his mouth, kissing a trail up her neck. Then he pulled away, and said, "Do you want to continue this in the bedroom?" He enjoyed a good make-out session, but Kaity was hot and he wanted to keep exploring her.

She lifted a hand from his hair, and swiped it across her cheek. Then she smiled sheepishly at him. "Yes, let's," she murmured, rising from where she'd been straddling him. He also stood, briefly adjusting his pants, and he let her take the lead.

Chapter 23

A little unsteady on her feet, Kaity pulled Gabe into her bedroom. The lamp by the bed was on, ensuring that it was not too light and not too dark. She was about to do a quick scan to see if she'd left anything embarrassing out, but then she felt Gabe guiding her to the bed.

"How will you be most comfortable?" he asked.

Kaity felt like she was already flushed, or else she would've blushed at the memory that she'd already told him that she'd fallen on her butt earlier that day. She sank down onto the bed, landing on her side, with her head at the headboard, stretched out long. Gabe mirrored her position, and then he was pulling her close to keep kissing her.

She retreated after another breathless kiss.

"Wait, why are you still wearing a shirt?" she asked playfully. Surprise sparked his eyes, and Kaity had to smile at that. Maybe it had been a while since she'd done anything spontaneous, if it was that obvious to other people.

Gabe pulled away in order to pull the long-sleeved shirt over his head; it had stretched to accommodate the motion, even though there were a few ornamental buttons on it. Now that she got a chance to look, she decided that he had a nice body. He was lean, a little muscled, more tan than her. They were laying far enough apart that she could reach in a hand to trail it up his chest, encountering a little bit of chest hair.

"Mmm," Gabe breathed. He had been propping himself up on one elbow, and with this exhalation he let his head fall onto Kaity's pillow. She continued to run her hand up and down his chest, watching him rest his head, his brown curls splayed out against the lavender pillow case.

After a few moments, he picked himself back up, and nuzzled close to Kaity, his lips finding hers so that they were making out again. He was clean shaven, so there wasn't any stubble to burn when he broke the kiss to slide down her neck, kissing there, and then slide down further to kiss her breasts again.

Kaity couldn't help it: it felt so good and it'd been so long that her hips began tilting and tucking on their own, seeking closeness and stimulation. Embarrassed, she pulled away a little. What had she just been saying to Anabelle about not throwing herself at the first guy post-divorce who'd looked twice at her?

"Hey," Gabe said, cupping her cheek and bringing their faces close together again. "You okay? Does this feel good?"

Kaity made a sound approximating "murrr." Then she felt even more self-conscious, so she flipped onto her other side, putting her back to Gabe. As she moved, she thought she felt a bit more slide than usual between her thighs.

He hugged her from behind, aligning his body with hers, and doing it slowly and gently so that he didn't jar her bruised butt. She felt his face in her hair, and felt his breath as he started to speak.

"If we need to slow down, that's fine," he murmured. "But in case you were wondering, you're gorgeous, and I think you deserve some pleasure."

Kaity arched back into him a little. Her butt was sensitive from the fall, but that made everything feel more intense, in a good way.

"I like this," she managed to get out. "It's just...been a while. And I'm...self-conscious because of things my ex said."

Gabe just held her, and then began nosing around in her hair until his lips found the back of her neck. He kissed her there, and whispered: "We can take it slow. And your ex is a douche. You're gorgeous."

Kaity let out a small, whimpering exhale. Somehow this felt so *good*. She reminded herself that this didn't have to be forever, that she could explore feeling sexy on her own terms, that Gabe had already shown himself to be a nice person.

"Thank you," she said. And then, "don't stop kissing me."

He kissed the back of her neck, and then gently nibbled around that same area. His hands found her breasts, cupping and squeezing them. Unsure what to do with her hands, Kaity draped them over his busy hands. She noticed that she was squirming a bit, though, so she let one hand move downward, until her palm was on her belly, with her fingertips gliding lower. She touched the top of her clit through her thin joggers, and felt warmth radiating out. She reached down a bit more, confirming what she'd suspected earlier: she was already wet. The last few pathetic times she'd had sex in her marriage, she'd barely gotten wet at all, leading to lube use, which her ex had taken as a personal affront.

The kissing at her neck had stopped, and she looked back over her shoulder to see Gabe lifting himself up to look down at her.

"Don't stop on my account," he said, glancing down at where her hand was.

Kaity squirmed. She was no stranger to masturbation, but in front of someone?

He must have sensed her discomfort, because he said, "If it feels good, I want you to do it. Both because it'll make you feel good, and because it might give me some useful tips for later." He flashed a grin at her, and then buried his teeth in her shoulder, not enough to draw blood, but definitely enough to send a jolt down her spine.

Twitching with the aftershocks of that sensation, and reassured by his statement, Kaity resumed touching herself. One of Gabe's hands joined her, nestling over her hand, not guiding it so much as riding along to feel what she liked.

He kept kissing the back of her neck. Her breath hitched. She could feel her hips rocking, tilting and tucking to meet their hands. Gabe could feel it too, and he whispered into her neck. "Keep touching yourself, beautiful." She shuddered.

Kaity could feel herself getting closer, and all thoughts of self-conscious self-monitoring left her mind. She pushed her butt back into Gabe, feeling his hardness through both their pants. Her rhythmic breathing grew louder, and turned into a moan. The sensations built, and Gabe whispered similar-sounding things in her ear, calling her beautiful and encouraging her to touch herself.

With a cry, lost in Gabe's hands and mouth on her, Kaity came. The climax rolled over her like a wave, and she continued to breathe hard for a few moments. She'd stilled her hand, and Gabe's hand over hers had gone still as well, though he pressed down through his palm. The small amount of pressure had caused her orgasm to resonate through the area, sending shockwaves through her body.

Gabe lifted his lips from her neck and mouthed, "Feel good?"

Not trusting herself to speak yet, Kaity nodded. "Good," was one thing...blissed out was another, and way closer to how she felt right now. Gabe continued to hold her while she returned to herself.

Eventually, she lifted her head and turned to look at him, finding his gaze locked on her, a wolfish smile on his lips.

"I could do this all day," he murmured. The words surprised Kaity, and she disliked that her first thought had been that he would ask for his turn to be pleasured. But then, the five years she'd been married to her ex would have granted him ample time for that kind of behavioral conditioning. Maybe it was time to lay some new mental pathways.

She turned onto her other side, facing Gabe, and laced her fingers around the back of his neck. She looked him in the eye; he appeared to be honest in his enjoyment of their activities. His bottom hand stayed trapped where it was, and his top hand drifted down her side to clench her hip. "Nothing hurts, right?" he asked. She shook her head.

"I just need to catch my breath," she said. Gabe wriggled his bottom arm free and used that hand to stroke her cheek.

"Totally fine," he said. "I'll grab myself a glass of water, if that's okay?" Kaity rose up, intending to do it herself, but he gently pushed her back down on the bed.

"Okay," she said weakly. "Bring me one too?" He grinned and nodded, and stood, letting Kaity enjoy the view of him walking away, shirtless. Then she flopped back down on her back, for once simply enjoying the moment.

Chapter 24

K aity was disrupted from her reverie when Gabe came back, bearing two glasses of water.

She'd been laying on her back, topless, lost in the full-body distributed pleasure that was oddly similar to the feeling after a good workout. Feeling like a sweaty mess was one thing in common between the two states. Caring about what others thought of her during these activities: that was less of a thing over time.

"Hey," he said as he entered the room, getting her attention. She propped herself up on one elbow, admiring the view.

"Thanks." She reached for the glass of water and drank deeply before setting it on the nightstand. He took a sip of his, then set it down as well.

Then Gabe climbed back into—well, onto—the bed with her, and also propped himself up on one elbow, mirroring her posture. He lifted a hand to stroke her hair, starting at the temple and working down, grazing her neck as well.

"You are beautiful," he said, "and for you to have been with someone who didn't regularly tell you that is criminal neglect."

Kaity ducked her head and giggled. "You're not so bad-looking yourself."

"You have to trust me on this, I have an artist's eye," Gabe replied, looking humorously affronted.

Kaity lifted her head so that her eyeroll would be visible.

"I will keep saying this kind of thing until you shut me up," Gabe warned her. She wasn't sure how far to interpret his words, but she decided to go for it, propelling herself forward for another deep kiss. On the one hand, she felt sated, moreso than she had in a while...on the other hand, she felt curious and playful, again, moreso than she had in a while.

She kept kissing Gabe, again exploring his mouth with her tongue, and slowly rolling onto him so that their chests were pressed together. The pressure on her breasts felt good, and once they were fully situated with him on his back, he put his hands on her hips, squeezing and touching her there. He was, she noted, extremely gentle whenever his hands grazed her butt, in deference to her fall.

She pulled back to catch her breath, and Gabe said, "As I was saying..." Kaity laughed and went back for another kiss, rubbing her breasts on him. He was taller than her, so their hips were not aligned in this position, but she could feel him moving a bit underneath her. Now that she was thinking of his hips, the idea to explore the area occurred to her.

Kaity broke off the kiss, but took two fingers and inserted them into Gabe's mouth. He began sucking on them, in a way that made Kaity wish he were exploring other parts of her with his tongue. Then she slid down his chest slowly, kissing him there, and kept going until she reached his beltline. She placed kisses along its edges, and felt Gabe moan into her fingers.

Lifting her eyes to meet his gaze, Kaity saw adoration and hunger there. It felt different. It felt good. She decided to keep exploring.

She withdrew her fingers to help with unbuckling his belt and unzipping his jeans, and Gabe panted instead of talking. She freed him from his pants and underwear, and began to gently touch and stroke him. He groaned softly, and Kaity watched his face for signs of what he might enjoy. At this stage, however, it seemed like he enjoyed everything...and that he enjoyed her.

She looked down, and found the sight appetizing, and doubled over in order to start kissing up and down his shaft. Gabe's breathing intensified, and Kaity could feel her body responding too, even though she'd just pleasured herself.

She stopped before taking him fully into her mouth, feeling stupid. The divorced ladyfriends group had hired a sex educator to do a workshop on safe hook-up sex, and she'd skipped over the part that the educator had emphasized as important: the safer sex talk, which was supposed to happen before people started getting naked.

"Gabe?" she asked. His lovely brown eyes went from half-closed to her face. "Do you...?" she wasn't quite sure how to phrase it.

"I have a condom with me," he answered. Which was a decent enough answer, but not the entirety of what she was looking for.

She pulled back a little more, so that she wouldn't be asking this with her face in his crotch.

"Oh, okay. Cool. What I meant is, I'm sorry, do you ever get tested for STIs?" The words tumbled out. Feeling hideously awkward already, she decided to keep going and hope she didn't ruin the mood, despite the sex educator's emphatic insistent that talking about safer sex did not ruin the mood, and any moods it ruined were crappy and unsustainable moods to begin with. "I did after my divorce, and I haven't been with anyone since then, so, ummm..."

Gabe blinked. The pause before he spoke made Kaity reconsider the optimistic stance she'd taken regarding "ruining the mood." A chill threatened to rove her body.

Then he smiled, and she felt a little melty with the combination of relief and post-orgasmic happy chemicals.

"I've gotta hand it to you for attention to details," he said. "Yeah, I was tested a few months ago, and I always use condoms."

Kaity deliberately steered her brain away from analyzing the gaps in that sentence, since she'd retained a lot of information from the sex educator's workshop. But that could be a discussion for another time, if there was another time. Tonight, she just wanted to feel alive and immerse herself in someone tasty.

So instead of saying anything else awkward, Kaity leaned down and took him into her mouth.

Gabe was tickled by Kaity's sensible questions. Then he was distracted by her mouth. He refrained from gripping her hair, since he knew not every woman liked that. He'd have to ask later. Everything about her was just so...earnest. Refreshingly so.

She started using her tongue more, flicking it up and down as she gave him head, and Gabe could feel his hips beginning to flex more regularly. He wasn't sure if she was feeling done for the night or if sex was an option, so he gently drew her away.

Her eyes went wide, and Gabe realized that she thought she'd done something wrong. Yeah, her ex had definitely been a huge douche to instill that kind of response in her.

"That feels really good," he reassured her, "but I'll probably come if you keep going. Are you up for having sex?"

Eyes still wide, she nodded. Gabe drew her in for a kiss, and then used that moment to shift their positions, so that she was on her back and he was on his side facing her. He kept kissing her, and used his hands to tug her pants and panties down, revealing luscious hips. Then he kissed his way down her neck, lingering at her breasts. He put one hand on her thighs, tracing patterns. That hand moved up her thighs, to play with her clit a little, before teasing around her opening. She was still really wet, but he was guessing that she hadn't had sex in a while, so the more foreplay the better.

Kaity moaned softly and tossed her head back. That moment alone should have been a photo, he thought.

He slid a finger in, then withdrew it and played with the folds of labia. He noticed a series of tiny bruises on her inner thigh; one of the many delights of being a pole dancer, no doubt. He inserted a finger again, then two, and slowly pumped in and out. By the way she responded with more moans and the rocking of her hips, he wondered if she was one of those women who could have multiple orgasms.

"Kaity?" he asked, making sure his tone was soft. She looked at him, her eyes a bit unfocused. "Mm?"

"Do you want me inside you?"

She bobbed her head up and down in an emphatic nod. That was all Gabe needed. He found the pocket the condoms were in, shucked his pants off the rest of the way, and carefully opened the packet. He minimally unrolled it to make sure he had the right side, and then sheathed himself. Alex would be proud, he thought wryly, given that she'd taken it upon herself to give him all the sexual etiquette tips for safely and pleasurably hooking up with a woman.

Gabe returned his attention to Kaity, and found her looking at him a little apprehensively. He leaned in to kiss her and then whispered, "I won't hurt you."

As though that was exactly what she needed to hear, she reclined and gazed up at him with a small smile on her face. And then, as though she'd been holding onto this thought, she whispered back, "Good, because I've been hurt enough already. And I don't just mean my poor, bruised butt."

He chuckled, then kissed her, and started to ease his way on top of her. He guided himself in, and paused to make sure she was okay. She kept kissing him, and so he went the rest of the way in, and she clutched at his hips, crying out softly.

He stopped. "Keep going," she murmured. Gabe kissed her temples, which were a little sweaty, and then began to work up a rhythm. Soft and warm beneath him, Kaity reached up to grab his hair and guide him in for more kisses. Then she guided his head down to her neck. He obligingly kissed her there, causing her to arch her back. Being inside her felt good, really good, but Gabe wasn't satisfied with just one position. He withdrew from her abruptly, leading to a small vocalization of protest from her, and then he flipped onto his back, and smiled at her invitingly. Or so he hoped.

"Care to ride?" he asked, folding his arms behind his head in a waiting pose. Kaity exhaled, then nodded her head. She clambered on top of him, but instead of immediately easing him in, she paused. Gabe clamped his lips together, feeling his body strain towards hers. Slowly, Kaity lowered her hips to his, simply to rub herself up and down the length of him. The teasing sensation made him shiver with delight.

"Oh, did you mean now?" she asked, lifting both eyebrows. Gabe resolutely kept his arms behind his head, determined to enjoy this new playful side of her. She eventually reached a hand down to guide him in, and moaned a little once he was fully inside her. Gabe couldn't help himself, and reached his hands down to squeeze and caress her hips and thighs. She sat upright for a little bit, and then lowered herself forward, bracing against his chest as she rode him.

Gabe felt himself getting into a rhythm that would bring him close. He moved his hands fully onto Kaity's hips, so he could encourage her to stay with that rhythm. But then she switched it up, moving faster and with more urgency, and Gabe smiled at the suspicion that he was right, and she might come again.

And there it was—Kaity shuddering and moaning atop him, slowing the rhythm while she closed her eyes and gasped for breath. Gabe felt his own arousal building, and he whispered to her, "Can you handle some more?" In answer, she flopped over onto her side, pulling him out in the process. Gabe checked the condom and moved to spoon her, guiding himself back in. Kaity still seemed to be in the intense aftermath of her own orgasm, so he started slow, and built back up to the rhythm he enjoyed. He fondled her breasts, pounding into her while he got closer.

Being inside her felt *so good*, and as he felt the warmth building in his groin, he moaned low and long, building towards release. Then he only heard their flesh slapping together, felt the pulse as he came inside her.

He slowed his frantic pace with a few twitches, both in his hips and in his fingertips, which had ranged all over her body.

He wasn't sure if he had the words to explain how good she felt, so he stayed silent for a few moments.

"Did you come?" Kaity whispered.

"Yeah, did you?"

She chuckled. "Yeah, a second time. I wasn't sure if it'd happen, it doesn't happen very often for me."

Gabe kissed her shoulder, and the two of them stayed entwined in silence for a bit, before he pulled out, making sure to support the condom at its base. He didn't have to look far to find a trash can, and then he returned to bed, pulling Kaity close. He had to admit, she was more fun in bed than he'd thought initially, given how restrained and shy she seemed. He wondered if he'd get to keep exploring her like this, and planted some more kisses on her shoulders while she seemed lost in thought.

Chapter 25

Kaity felt so relaxed that she caught herself almost dozing off, nestled in Gabe's arms atop her askew bedspread and sheets. Then she remembered that she was supposed to do something...what was it, that's right, pee after sex to prevent urinary tract infections. There was no sexy way to say that, so she got up and excused herself to go to the bathroom.

She had a robe to put on, so she did, and she reveled in the feeling of silk against her skin. She had never thought of herself as a particularly sensual person, sensible was more the word for her, but today was apparently just full of surprises.

When she returned to her bedroom, she found that Gabe had worked his way under the covers. He was laying on his back, some chest exposed, hands behind his head. He looked over when she entered the room, and smiled.

"Hi, beautiful," he said. She blushed and ducked her head in return, though there was really no reason to be shy at this point. So instead, she shucked the robe and crawled back into bed. His arms welcomed her, and she nuzzled his shoulder.

"That was fun," she whispered.

"Agreed," he replied.

Kaity remained still and cocooned for a few more minutes, then said, "I think I need to get up and do some things before I go to sleep." Besides, she didn't necessarily want him spending the night; she'd grown accustomed to sleeping alone.

Thankfully Gabe got the hint, and he stretched out long, then got up and started searching for his clothes. Kaity propped herself up on one elbow and watched him dress.

"Do you ever model?" she asked. He gave a startled laugh.

"No, but thanks for the compliment. I prefer to be behind the camera."

She decided to be bold. "Well, *I* think you're plenty good-looking."

He returned to where she was laying, and dropped to his knees to give her a long kiss. Kaity couldn't help but lean into it, wanting more even as her body was beginning to protest fitting so much into one day. He broke off the kiss, and caressed her face with one hand, the other hand clutching his shirt.

"You are just too sweet," he murmured. Kaity squirmed a little. Apparently her body wasn't *that* tired. He rose and finished dressing.

"You going to be okay on your own? No need for further massage or attention?"

Kaity got up and put her robe back on. "Yes, thank you. I'll see you out." She walked him to the door, where he paused for another kiss before leaving.

Then Kaity remembered she hadn't really had dinner, and so once she'd heated up a freezer meal and made another cup of tea, she sank down into her loveseat with her phone. Anabelle had already texted her to check in post-fall and see if she was doing okay. There was also some sort of suggestion about DIY blended margaritas and using the excess ice to ice down her butt. When Kaity replied to relay what had happened, Anabelle had typed in a string of exclamation points. At that point, Kaity decided to switch to a phone conversation.

After Anabelle had demanded details, which Kaity mostly relayed, there was a pause.

"But what about your work party?"

Kaity's stomach dropped. That Trader Mo's stir fry bowl no longer felt like a good idea.

"I...hadn't thought about that. Oh my god."

"Kaity, that isn't like you...are you sure you're uninjured from your fall? No concussion or anything?"

That got a laugh out of Kaity. "You saw me! I just fell on my butt and scared myself. No, I guess I just felt spooked, and wanted to feel alive. And seeing Gabe was a good way to do that...um, not that I was using him. He *definitely* enjoyed himself."

"So you think your fake relationship is still on? Even though you just had real sex?"

Kaity sighed. Trust Anabelle to always ask the hard questions.

"I don't know. I guess I'll talk to him tomorrow."

"Well, good luck. I'm glad you had a good time though...I think it's generally a great idea to have some fun sexy-times where you're not necessarily too attached, just as a reminder that even though our exes were jerks, there are still some nice guys out there."

"I guess so?" Kaity wasn't sure what she thought of that statement; it wasn't like she was intending to get into a relationship anytime soon. She hadn't really thought about what she wanted after her divorce, instead staying focused on the logistics of creating a life for herself: job, apartment, a few friends. If she needed or wanted anything beyond that, well, that was news to her.

And it's not like any of her life here had any permanence. She could pack up her apartment as easy as a wish and be out in an afternoon. Nothing had really changed since her divorce other than where she lived, so it was likely that she'd be asking to end her lease early and move back to Louisville.

She wound down her chat with Anabelle and decided not to worry about any of the upcoming events. She'd figure out what to do about her work party, and call her apartment office in the morning. And she'd enjoy the memories of her time with Gabe as just one more nice thing in her life, like a cup of hot, fragrant tea cupped in her hands on a cold day.

Gabe had texted Alex to grab a meal and a beer, and so they found themselves at Maroon Street Tap House in SoBro. Gabe devoured a banh mi and then ordered another.

"Work up an appetite much, dude?" Alex had asked with a knowing smile.

After a sip of his coffee stout, Gabe answered: "Yeah, we *definitely* had a good time."

Alex raised an eyebrow, her signal that she was curious but respected the privacy of Gabe (and his female partners) too much to directly ask for details.

"So," Gabe said, "I think you were right about Kaity. She's into me, since she texted me after she'd had a fall in pole class. She's okay and everything, just shaken up, so I guess that prompted her to want to hook up."

"Ah," Alex said, nodding knowingly, her blond ponytail bobbing. "The moment when one realizes one's mortality, and then wants to taste life even more deeply."

"Very deep, my friend. So, I tried to go slow since I got the impression that her ex said some stuff that messed her up, and she probably hadn't had sex in a while. And you know what, it wasn't as hard as I'd thought to slow down and really pay attention to her pleasure, since she looks really hot in those moments." He half-smiled, remembering touching Kaity while she touched herself.

"Okay, so a good time was had by all. Are you guys still planning on keeping things casual?"

Gabe took another sip of his beer. "Haven't had the talk yet. She seems like the kind of person who doesn't walk on the wild side, so probably we'll have a little more sex, she'll say she's interested in a relationship, I'll say I'm not, and we'll go back to being friends."

Alex propped her chin on her fist and looked at Gabe. He imagined his hair was still sex-ruffled. And Kaity had suggested that he was handsome enough to model, ha! He knew he was good-looking, but it wasn't like he had much else to offer in a relationship, even if someone held his interest for that long.

"This is just my opinion," Alex said slowly, "but I think Kaity is a good catch and that she'd be good for you, like, long-term."

Gabe playfully elbowed Alex. That was easier than considering the cold feeling in his stomach, that he could've seriously messed things up by going too fast with Kaity. "Oh come on, we're just having fun. You know I'm halfway married to my work anyway."

Alex rolled her eyes. "Fine, you do you, man. Invite her out next time, though. I like her, and I think we could find some local brews that she'd enjoy." Gabe nodded to get Alex to shut up, even as he seriously doubted that Kaity would want to come hang with them as bros. Besides, that might give her the wrong idea about him having long-term interest, which he most definitely did not.

Chapter 26

Kaity woke up feeling energized despite not getting quite enough sleep, and she decided that it was only a one-travel-mug-of-tea kind of day.

She strode into the office with a sense of quiet calm and purpose. Maybe her personal life was a bit of a mess, but she could just move back to Louisville in over a month and be done with all this. She'd drive back to Mariontown once a month or so, see friends like Anabelle, and reminisce about the good times they'd had. Then she could drive home to Louisville and build the life there that her marriage and subsequent move and divorce had disrupted.

As eleven am rolled around, Kaity found herself anxiously checking her phone. Was it hook-up protocol to text a "hey, I had fun with you" the morning after? Or the afternoon? Or even wait a day so as not to look desperate? No, longer than a day would indicate lack of interest...and Kaity was definitely interested in a repeat. Or two. Or three.

She decided to rummage for snacks or drinks in the shared lounge/kitchen area.

Georgia was sulking in a chair when Kaity walked in, and shot her a gaze of spoiled fruit: sweet, but too sweet, and rotten if you looked too closely.

Kaity ignored her and walked to the fridge. She felt Georgia's eyes on her back as she opened it, found a bottled cold brew, and withdrew it.

Deliberately, Kaity turned around and stared into Georgia's frosty blue eyes.

"Don't you, like, have a life?" Kaity inquired. She meant to sound arch, but probably she sounded a bit worn around the edges. Having sex well into the night did that to a person.

Georgia scoffed, but averted her eyes. And then she stood and left the room.

Kaity was puzzled but, as she later told Anabelle, completely fine with that outcome. Any day when Georgia wasn't aiming barbs at her was a good one, even if her reasons for backing down were inscrutable to the human eye. Come to think of it, she couldn't recall a time when Georgia had been the first one to look away during a confrontation.

Thoroughly caffeinated and back at her desk, Kaity realized that had a solution to the "to text or not to text" problem. It involved a quick errand, and then texting.

Gabe was pleasantly surprised to hear from Kaity as he worked on yet another batch of wedding photos. He hadn't decided whether or not he was within the "too soon" window to text her back yet, so it was with a small side of relief that he read her invitation to come over again that very night.

Well, he thought, if it's going to be a fun and sexy fling, we're off to the right start.

That thought was quickly followed by an appreciation of the irony that he was doing his best to avoid a committed relationship, while editing photos which celebrated precisely that. Although, if he ever did get married, his step-mom would likely view it as a positive sign of maturity and let him see Holly more. As though that'd happen before she turned eighteen and could make her own choices. And as though Marcia wouldn't just try to ingratiate herself with whomever he married to try to sway her in various matters.

Gabe sighed. Family: you couldn't live with them, you couldn't live without them. Since he now had evening plans, he opted for ramen for lunch, instead of going out. Another delightful day in the life of a working artist.

But at least the evening held some promise of delight.

Since it was Tuesday, Kaity didn't have either of her dance classes, so she was able to come home after work and eat her normal early dinner...and get ready for her visit with Gabe. She fielded a few "you go, girl!" texts from Anabelle, and changed her sheets.

As she gathered the current set of lavender cotton sheets into her hands, she paused, running her fingertips along the material. Impulsively, she lifted the sheets to her face to smell them, and pulled back with a nose full of Gabe...Gabe and her, their scents intermingled. That action felt a bit more carnal than she usually was into, but it was also pleasurable, in a way that she was starting to embrace. It was as though six weeks of pole dance and a few weeks of rolling around on the floor had woken up parts of her body that she was accustomed to ignoring. Or maybe those parts of her had gone dormant when her marriage had soured.

But she could move on now. *Was* moving on now. She could explore being a sexier version of herself with Gabe, and enjoy her time at Snapdragon and with Anabelle, and then put all this behind her when she moved back to Louisville.

It's funny, she thought: being Gabe's stand-in girlfriend had led to them growing close enough to fall into bed together. And now having sex with him was just another form of practice, another way to fake it til she made it. Eventually she'd have a real relationship with someone, maybe even end up getting married again. Not that it had to be soon. But the part of her brain that liked meticulously planning things was already setting up a timeline: move back to Louisville in a month, get her own place, readjust to the Louisville branch of her work, maybe find a yoga or dance studio on her own and make her own friends there while reconnecting with her Louisville friends, maybe meet someone through them who was just right for her.

Kaity put new sheets on her bed, smoothing them with the palms of her hands. One hand snagged on the fine thread count, leading to a weird pulling sensation, and so she examined her hand: there were calluses dotting the palm. That was probably a normal thing to happen in pole dance, but Kaity made a mental note to get a manicure and have them shaved off when she got back to Louisville.

Next, Kaity lit some candles and put on something that she hoped was sexier than the joggers and soft tee she'd been wearing the previous night when Gabe had come over to comfort her: a red slip and matching robe. That had been a relic from her married days, in the "spice up your marriage to save it" phase she'd gone through (as had many of the divorced ladyfriends, subsequent conversations demonstrated). She'd never actually ended up wearing it with John, so it felt like it was fair to wear it with Gabe.

She got out the items she'd picked up on her lunch break, and was about to see who was texting her when there was a knock at the door. Clearly Gabe wasn't texting her if he was already here, so she could ignore those texts.

She intended to ignore everything but Gabe for a while, until it was time to move on with the rest of her life.

It seemed like as good a plan as any.

Chapter 27

Gabe knocked at Kaity's door. She hadn't asked him to bring anything, so he didn't...but he still wondered if he should be showing up empty-handed. What was the protocol for something like this with someone you were fake-dating but real-fucking?

She answered the door in a sexy but not overly revealing matching red slip and robe, indicating what was on the menu tonight. Her hair was down around her shoulder, which Gabe liked; he'd been drawn to seeing her hair undulating on her shoulders since that first photoshoot where he'd finally gotten her to relax.

Her face crinkled into a smile. "Hey, come on in." He found himself smiling in return. Other body parts of his warmed up as well.

She'd set up her small living room with candles instead of having any of the overhead lights on, and there was a trunk in place of the small coffee table, situated between the loveseat and one of the kitchen-table chairs.

On the trunk was a series of beer bottles and an assortment of mis-matched glasses, from pint glasses and wine glasses to mugs.

She caught his gaze lingering on the table and offered another smile. "I thought it'd be fun to do a beer tasting, so you could show me around some of your favorites. I also bought a few beers from Louisville that my friends there recommended."

Gabe walked to the trunk, and saw that there were indeed some of his favorites on it: Maroon Lane's house stout and Broad River Brewpub's imperial IPA. He didn't recognize the other two bottles, but he suspected they were at least decent quality based on the art on the labels.

He looked back to Kaity, who was smiling radiantly in her sexy get-up, and for a moment he was lost for language. He couldn't remember a time when anyone he'd dated had noticed or cared what his favorite beers were, even though hitting local breweries (especially with Alex) was one of his favorite pastimes. What did a thoughtful gesture like this mean if it came from someone he was explicitly not dating for real?

"Thank you," was what he settled on, and then he sat down in the loveseat. Kaity made to sit in the chair opposite the trunk, but Gabe reached out to tug her towards him instead, settling her on his lap. She giggled, probably a surprise response of hers, Gabe noted.

"Okay so...do you like beer at all? If so, which kinds of beer?" Gabe knew his palate was not the same as a friendly starter set. However, Kaity surprised him by explaining that she'd discovered a great liking for amber ales in her marriage, and had explored a great deal of the Louisville breweries when with her ex-husband. Well, at least one good thing had come out of that marriage, Gabe mused. That, and Kaity moving to Mariontown.

He walked her through his two faves, unsurprised when she made a face at the bitterness of both the stout and the imperial IPA. The flavors did open up on subsequent sips, he advised, and she humored him and tried subsequent sips, agreeing with his assessment. The two beers she'd selected from Louisville breweries were a porter and an amber, and he found that he liked them well enough. And there was really no beating a beer tasting with a good-looking woman in his lap.

He told Kaity this, and she squirmed a little, then set her glass down and twisted around to kiss him. He kissed her back, and soon they were full-on making out. He took advantage of her back being mostly to him and started running his hands up and down her silk-clad torso, pausing to fondle her breasts. This made her gasp, and he could feel her beginning to grind a little on his thigh. Between that and her hands in his hair, tugging to punctuate the kisses, he felt his desire grow.

Gabe broke off the kiss to twist Kaity all the way around to face him, and then he lifted her up as he stood. She squeaked a bit. But she wrapped her legs around him, which allowed him to carry her to the bedroom. When he set her down on the bed, he saw that her face was a little pale.

"Um, should I have asked first?" he said.

She shook her head. "No, it's just... I thought I was too heavy for anyone to pick up easily."

Gabe laughed. She narrowed her eyes at him. "I'm sorry, it's not funny, except... you're not the first woman to say that to me. I don't know where you get these hang-ups." Well, he had at least one guess: her crappy ex-husband.

Kaity drew her knees into her chest. Gabe noted that he'd clearly said the wrong thing, so he got down onto the bed with her and tried to cuddle her. She pulled away.

"Hey, sorry, I didn't mean to make light of that." Gabe's heart dully thudded in his chest, desire ebbing as he wondered whether he'd fucked up. It wasn't like he should care...but he did.

With her head still turned away from him, Kaity said, "I know this isn't a real relationship. But are you seeing anyone else right now?"

"No," Gabe said, and he was being honest. The dry spell was a bit annoying, but he knew he was working long hours, and he couldn't blame most women for not wanting to put up with his unavailability. God, it wasn't like he ever invited anyone back to his place, either; Alex and Johnny B both teased him about it being a bachelor pad, but he knew his apartment wasn't exactly welcoming.

The silence dragged on. Gabe contemplated leaving, since this seemed to be getting complicated.

Kaity finally turned to face him. "Good. Me too." Then she reached for him and kissed him, and Gabe was set aflame with desire all over again.

He ran his hands up and down her body, and got the robe over one shoulder so he could pull the thin red strap of the slip down, and take one of her breasts into his mouth. He flicked her nipple with his tongue over and over again, feeling her stiffen and then melt under his grip. With one hand, he explored the hem of the slip, and slid his fingers up to find that she wasn't wearing any underwear.

Gabe made a small guttural noise without intending to, and released her breast from his mouth in order to dive under the slip and kiss her thighs, then taste between her legs. He used his tongue to give a few long licks, and then focused on her clit, finding the right rhythm and amount of pressure to make her squirm. Her fingers interlaced in his hair, and he decided that he really, really liked that. He could feel himself growing hard, and he reached down a hand to briefly adjust himself through his pants before returning his attention to Kaity.

She was moaning, and her hips were bucking, so he figured he was on the right track. He inserted one finger, then another, and stroked the textured area inside that probably corresponded to her G-spot.

"Don't stop," she gasped, and so he stayed the course with rhythm and pressure. Her muscles clenched up and clenched him as she came, and she panted for the duration of the spasms. Gabe's fingers were drenched to the knuckle, and he salivated at the thought of licking them.

Kaity's motions had stilled, so he figured it was safe to slowly withdraw his fingers. He reached up with his other hand to caress her cheek, and then gently grip it to make sure she was watching him as he licked his fingers that had been inside her. She deserved to know how tasty she was, since it seemed like at least one asshole in her life had deprived her of that pleasure.

What followed was a sweaty fuck-fest: Gabe cuddled her until she'd recovered somewhat, then checked in verbally, then retrieved a condom. She was still sensitive while he penetrated her, so she moaned, and her moans helped get him off faster than she would've liked. He brought her water and beer to choose from (after a few sips of stout himself), and returned to touching her, only to go through another two condoms and more positions than he could count. Kaity's face and bosom flushed, and her ass, bruised in a couple places from pole, also blushed scarlet from the impact when he fucked her from behind.

It was almost too much. It was just enough. After going through that third condom, Gabe collapsed with Kaity in a sweaty heap. She nestled her butt into his hips, playing little spoon to his big spoon, and he rained down kisses on her shoulder.

Eventually, she got up to use the bathroom, donning her slip and robe once more. Though he was totally sexed out and relaxed, at some point during her absence, he could've sworn he heard a knocking at her door.

Chapter 28

K aity ran cold water over her face after using the bathroom, not that it helped with the rosy sex flush that ran from her cheeks to the tops of her breasts.

She was preparing to return to bed when she heard something at her door...not quite a knock, maybe more of a rustle? Which was weird, since it had to be after 9 or 10pm, but she decided to go check who it was anyway.

She tied the robe, ensuring that it was less revealing, and opened her front door.

Anabelle stood there, a package in one hand and a piece of white paper in the other. Her eyes were round, her face taut.

"What are you doing here?" Kaity asked.

"I texted to see if I could come drop this off," Anabelle said, lifting the hand with the package. "I ordered you a fishnet bodysuit. It came in today. I figured I could leave it on your doorstep if you weren't around."

"Okay...?" Kaity said. She didn't want to venture too far outside her door, dressed as she was, but Anabelle was hanging back a bit oddly, as though she hesitated to get close enough to Kaity to touch her.

"Then I saw this. It's from your apartment management." Anabelle held the paper out just enough for Kaity to take it from her hand.

It was the confirmation that she was ending her lease early, though the form specified that with an additional fee within one week the lease could still be followed through with and subsequently renewed at the same rent.

"Oh," Kaity murmured.

"When were you planning on telling me? Telling us?" Anabelle asked, her voice shaking.

"I...I just..." Kaity stopped and sighed. "I haven't been happy here."

"That's because you haven't been trying! So you're leaving!" Anabelle's voice rose. "You have friends here. You have a lover here. You have a job. Sure, your shitty ex and his bitchy sister are here too, but they're not your whole life! Your job isn't your whole life!"

Kaity noticed the tears in Anabelle's eyes, and the angry flush that contorted her normally cheerful and cute face. Her eyes began to burn in response; of all the people in her life, she'd never wanted to hurt Anabelle, or even anticipated that things would've gone this way.

"I was going to tell you," she started to say. The words fell flat, and she realized that she hadn't told anyone, and hadn't been planning on it. It'd been her perfect little plan, a tiny map of the future that belonged just to her.

"I haven't been happy here," she repeated.

"Yeah? Looks like you had a terrible time tonight," Anabelle shot back at her.

Kaity recoiled, tears truly forming in her eyes. "This isn't a real relationship. It's transient, like everything else here has been for me."

"It's only transient because you treated it that way," Anabelle countered. She darted forward to set the package inside the apartment door, at Kaity's feet. "I thought we were better friends than that. And I thought you were actually trying to move forward after your divorce, not stay stuck in the past, tethered to a city where you don't even live anymore. Do you have friends there? Do you have a dance studio there? Or a cute rebound?"

As Anabelle talked, Kaity felt more tears prick her eyes, and felt her shoulders slump. What had happened to her normally joyful, smiling friend? The friend who had opened her arms to Kaity along with other divorced women, and helped them find new hobbies and social groups?

"I'm sorry," Kaity ground out. "This is just how it is."

"It's how you *chose* for things to be," Anabelle retorted. She swiped a hand angrily across her face, wiping away tears. Her face stayed a mottled red, brightly contrasting with her blond hair. Then she backed away, still sniffling, and left.

Kaity stood in her doorway, feeling her heart pounding, before she remembered what she was wearing and stepped back inside, closing the door. Thankfully, it didn't seem like any of her neighbors were up and about this late; no one had stuck their heads out of their doors to see what the ruckus was.

She turned to go back to the bedroom, and saw Gabe in the doorway, wearing only a pair of jeans. He was leaning forward, bracing his hands on either side of the doorframe. The pose seemed mildly aggressive, until Kaity caught sight of his face.

He looked shattered.

Kaity felt like her stomach was dropping out as she realized that he'd overheard some or all of the conversation; enough, at any rate, to overhear that she was leaving.

Neither of them spoke for a long moment.

Finally, he said, in a voice so soft she could barely hear him: "So you're leaving." It wasn't a question.

Her already-warmed skin felt too hot, like a vise. Nervous, she nodded.

"If you weren't telling your best friend, I must not have been very high on the list." Gabe dropped his gaze, then lifted it again, searching Kaity's eyes. She didn't know what he was looking for, but she steeled herself to meet his gaze.

"I didn't mean to hurt you," Kaity said defensively.

"Oh, you think after hooking up twice I'm so into you that this hurts?" Gabe said, his tone clipped.

Kaity crossed her arms over her chest, tight, and then tighter, as though she could cover up her body, the parts of herself he had just enjoyed and pleasured.

"Look, I know you have abandonment issues—" she started.

"You barely know anything about me, " Gabe hissed, cutting her off.

Kaity backed up, startled. Dropped her arms from her chest, then picked them back up when she realized her breasts were about to fall out of her slip. This was something sex couldn't fix.

"I told you the barest outline of it, " Gabe continued, maintaining a distance from her. "My mom and brother died in a car crash. And do you know when they died? After picking me up from junior prom because I was devastated when my date didn't show. My mom told me she'd always be there for me, that it probably wasn't this girl's fault, that I should always be good to women no matter what. That I was going to be a good role model for my younger brother. And then we got into an accident, and I was the only one to walk away from it."

"I'm sorry," Kaity whispered.

Gabe dropped his eyes, and dropped his arms from the doorframe. He disappeared into her bedroom, and came back with his shirt and socks over one arm.

Kaity's heart began to ache from how long he didn't look at her. She started to say something, anything, and he glared at her then. "You don't know me, Kaity. But you've become one more reason why I can't let anyone in. Because everyone eventually leaves." The protest died in her throat, because of course he was right, she was about to leave, and she hadn't given a single thought to how it might impact him, or anyone.

He put on his shirt and socks, and walked past Kaity, not touching her, to locate and put on his shoes. He ran his hands through his hair, then checked his pockets.

A pause in his motions, followed by a sharp exhale. He looked at her once more, his gaze cold. "Run back home. Have a nice life there." Then he turned and let himself out.

Kaity stared after him in shock. Then sobs overtook her, and she sank onto the loveseat, reaching wildly around until she found a fuzzy blanket that she could pull over herself. It wasn't as good as Gabe's touch, but little was. Even if it'd just been some kind of rebound fling. Even if she'd guaranteed through her actions that he'd want nothing to do with her after this.

Just like Anabelle.

Just like her ex-husband.

Kaity buried her head in the blanket and cried, feeling her breath hitch and snot run down her nose. Just an hour ago she'd been having one of the sexiest encounters of her life, and now she'd made the mistake of trying to have it all: reconstructing what she'd liked of her old life while sampling the fun parts of her new life. Stupid to think she could've made it work here in Mariontown, a place tainted by her divorce. Stupid to want anything at all, stupid to care about others enough so that they could hurt her.

Kaity wound herself up in her soft blanket and cried until she felt spent, cried until she had no tears left in her, just shame and sorrow. And the knowledge that, somehow, it was on her to try to fix this, unless running away was truly what she wanted. She didn't know anymore. She just didn't know.

Chapter 29

K aity used a personal day the next day at work; always the careful planner, she had a few personal days saved up at any given time. And if this wasn't an emergency, what was?

She'd gone back to bed after calling in, and dozed for another hour. But her body had gotten used to waking up, and it'd gotten used to movement and various activities being a part of her days. So she got herself out of bed, made tea, and made almond croissants from a freezer package. While those were baking, she unrolled an old yoga mat and went through some of the warm-up motions and stretches that she remembered from her classes. Passing through a squat, she felt a little tingly and sore, and she blushed to remember how much sex she'd had the night before, before it all came crashing down.

Croissant in hand, she worked on composing an apology to Anabelle, but the more elaborate the words became, the less truthful it felt. The truth was that she was hurting, and she was afraid to come out of her shell and care too much for others, because if you cared about people it gave them the power to hurt you. And there was no good way to fit all that into a text message without sounding like a coward, so Kaity gave up and simply texted, "I'm sorry."

Then she put her phone away and took a long bath.

Out of the bath, and no response yet. She wondered if she should apologize to Gabe; this was in the same ambiguous realm as the question of how soon one should text after a fun first date, or in their case, a fun first hook-up.

Kaity tossed her phone onto her still-unmade bed, and then in her bathrobe, flopped down beside it. It was rare that she didn't make her bed, but this was apparently one of those days. She'd been worried that she wouldn't be able to sleep, with the scent of Gabe still on the sheets, but she'd fallen into a deep, dreamless slumber.

She wondered what Gabe was doing today, then mentally chastised herself for the thought. She reminded herself that he'd basically told her it was just sex, and he'd insinuated that hooking up twice wasn't enough to get him attached. Not that she wanted him attached. He was probably just looking for casual sex anyway, and there'd be a new girl in his bed tonight. Even though Kaity was just planning to leave, she did not find that thought reassuring.

The temptation to lounge around the apartment and spend all day absorbed in self-pity was tempting, but Kaity decided to only allot half a day to it. Around 12:30pm, she got dressed and went to the new cafe in SoBro that she'd visited once.

The good-looking gentleman was once again behind the counter, and he smiled when he saw her come in.

"Good afternoon! Welcome! What can I get for you today?"

Kaity dredged up a smile, hoping she didn't look as awful as she felt.

"Do you have any lunch specials?"

"No specials today, but please look over the menu and let me know what you'd like."

Kaity took the laminated menu from his hands, noting the warmth in his nut-brown skin. She'd felt cold ever since Gabe had left; the bath had just been a temporary reprieve.

In the mood for comfort food, Kaity ordered a pair of tea sandwiches, one cucumber with cream cheese and the other ham and cheese. Then she ordered a whole pot of loose-leaf tea, an afternoon ceylon that the proprietor recommended.

While waiting for the food and tea, Kaity got out her e-reader, but mostly stared into the distance. She watched the cars go by on College Ave, and she looked at all the paintings and portraits in the tea shop, many of which had an old-timey feel to them, reminiscent of old daguerreotypes. The opportunity to apply a highly specific photography word just made her think of Gabe, though, so she decided to find something on her e-reader that seemed worth reading.

Nothing immediately leaped out at her, and she remembered a conversation on the divorced ladyfriends group chat that had been about borrowing ebooks from the local public library, how it was free and there was a fantastic selection. Kaity sighed. One more thing she'd messed up; she'd never gotten around to checking out the libraries in this town, at first because the move to

Mariontown had kept her so busy (because of course she'd wrangled more of the logistics than her ex had, because she was just "better" at those kinds of things), and then the divorce had eaten up her time and energy, and then she'd slid from trying to settle in to her new place to trying to escape it.

"Here you are." The voice coming from behind Kaity startled her at first, but it was just the tea shop proprietor with her tea and sandwiches. "I already stopped the tea from steeping further, so it should be perfectly brewed. Just let me know if you'd like anything to go in it."

"Thank you," Kaity said, putting her e-reader aside. She'd find something she could lose herself in later. For now, tea and lunch was just the right combination of things to shut off her brain.

Two hours later, Kaity was sobbing in her apartment again, and she wasn't even sure why.

Anabelle hadn't texted her back, Gabe hadn't texted her at all, and she'd only received a brief email from Antonio asking if she was okay and if she'd be back at work tomorrow. She wrote a reply reassuring him that she would be, making a mental note to still schedule the talk to ask to be transferred back to the Louisville branch.

Without work to structure her day, there weren't a lot of easy ways for her to tell the weekdays apart.

With a sinking feeling, Kaity realized that it was Wednesday, hence the evening when she should be in choreo class. She definitely didn't feel up to it, and besides, she and Anabelle were evidently not talking. Oh well. She could eat the expense if she had to. Classes at Snapdragon weren't cheap, but at least her class fees would go towards supporting a cool, locally-owned business.

She'd already had a bath, though, so how else was she to spend her evening? Kaity anxiously checked the clock a few more times as the class time drew near, feeling like she was forgetting something even though she knew that she probably wasn't welcome in the class, and she'd been plotting to up and leave anyway, so it's not like she was super attached to this one class.

When a knock sounded at her door, Kaity practically jumped out of her loveseat. Surely it wasn't Gabe. And it seemed like Anabelle regretted coming over unannounced, so why would she pull a repeat?

Wiping at her face with her knuckles to make sure she wasn't crying anymore, Kaity slunk to the door and opened it.

Miriam stood there, looking perfectly bored.

Chapter 30

K aity blinked at Miriam, taking in her penciled-in black eyebrows, her pallid and impassive face, and her dark scarlet lips. Staring down at her phone, she barely looked up when Kaity answered the door. She was in black shorts with fishnets underneath, gigantic black boots, and a maroon batwing sweater.

"What are you doing here?" Kaity asked, dumbfounded.

Miriam finally looked up from her phone.

"Anabelle asked me to come get you. She said she's still mad at you, but we need you for the choreo."

Kaity wasn't sure what to do with that information, though she dimly recalled spending the previous class working on a formation that incorporated all six of the dancers. Okay, time to bluff. "Um, sorry, but I'm dropping the class. I have more important things to do with my time."

Miriam glanced back down at her phone. "Anabelle said you'd say that. And no offense, but you're at home crying in your sweatpants, so precisely which important things are you doing right now?"

Damn, Anabelle had outmaneuvered her. And Miriam was perceptive, despite how much of an apathetic vibe she gave off.

Kaity sighed and held the door open. "Fine. I just need to find a sports bra. You can come in while I change."

Miriam walked in, a faint expression of distaste evident on her face. When Kaity returned to the living room from the bedroom, she caught Miriam still looking around, though admittedly there wasn't much to look at.

"You really haven't settled in here, have you?" Miriam asked, staring at all the blank walls.

"I haven't had time," Kaity said defensively.

"Look," Miriam said, finally meeting Kaity's eyes with her own. "Whatever happened between you and Anabelle is between the two of you. She asked me to bring you to class because your presence makes or breaks our group choreography. But I can look at your apartment and tell that you're running away from something. So you can either keep running away, or you come with me and run towards something for once."

With that, she turned around and walked towards the front door, swaying in her tall boots.

Momentarily stunned, Kaity paused to scoop up her gym bag and grab a water bottle before following. She wasn't sure if she'd just been subjected to a nihilistic pep talk or what, but she didn't want to disappoint multiple people in her life if she could help it.

"Gabe?"

He stirred, and felt something on his cheek. Rather, several things on his cheek.

They were hard, but not sharp. Patterned. Square.

He picked his head up from where he'd passed out over his keyboard, piecing together that he'd pulled an all-nighter, and it had ended poorly.

"Hey, man, I brought you coffee," Alex was saying. The sharp aroma reached his nose, and he reached out for the sweet nectar of life. But he was still slouched over his keyboard, so his hand didn't get very far. So he leveraged himself up to more of a sitting position, and found himself looking at Alex's very near and very concerned face.

"Urgh," Gabe said, and recoiled slightly. Alex put a coffee cup in his hand, then leaned back in the chair she'd borrowed, cradling her own coffee to her chest, sitting opposite him with a pensive expression on her face.

"Soooo," Alex said. "Last I heard things were going well. Then you texted me at—hang on, let me check—4am to invite me out for a beer, because you wanted me to commiserate with you about, and I quote, 'the fickleness of women, lust, and love.'"

Gabe groaned.

Alex gestured to Gabe's desk in his studio, and Gabe instantly regretted giving Alex a spare key. He regretted it in general, not right now because Alex had brought coffee, but also right now, because Alex was pointing out Gabe's series of beer cans, potato chip bags, water bottles, and the other detritus of an ill-considered all-nighter.

"Okay, so..." Gabe paused to take a pull of the coffee. It was good stuff, Mohnon Coffee Co, and he hoped it would go straight to his head and leave his stupid heart out of the equation.

"Okay, so," he started again, "I might have decided to lose myself in my work. It seemed like a good idea at the time. Kaity's leaving."

"And you're letting her?" Alex asked.

"It's not my fucking choice," Gabe shot back. He rubbed a hand on his cheek, hoping the keyboard marks would start to fade. "She had this plan to move back to Louisville the whole time, didn't tell anyone including her best friend, and then acted surprised when it blew up in her face." He sipped his coffee again. Anything to get the taste of Kaity out of his mouth.

"Oh, for fuck's sake," Alex said. Gabe looked over to see her rolling her eyes and shaking her head.

"What?" Gabe demanded. "I'm not allowed to be pissed off in this situation?"

"Yes, Gabe, your feelings are valid," Alex said in a matter-of-fact tone. "But you have to realize that you're just responding the way your emotional damage tells you to. Like yes, you're quite independent. And you like your life, and you like who you are. But ever since your mom's death you've been afraid of the people you love leaving you." She added in a rush, "...and for good reason! I was your friend back then too, and I saw how much it sucked for you. This is how you've been since then. And it's why Kaity's actions, which really have nothing to do with you, have hurt you so much."

Gabe told himself that Alex was one of his oldest friends, and hence she had a unique vantage point onto his emotional landscape. He told himself that, and it didn't help.

"Stay out of my head," he muttered, and then tried to insert as much coffee into his mouth in one gulp as possible.

Alex cocked her head, then shook it. "Look, my dude, you can sulk for as long as you want. I'll be here when you want to come out of your cave. It's up to you how much you want to let the patterns from your past determine how you react in the present."

She pushed herself into a standing position, and gestured with her coffee to the door. "I'll see myself out. Let me know when you want to talk. It'll be your turn to get coffee, too."

Gabe managed to stay upright while Alex walked out of his studio, locking the door behind her. He avoided slumping back down over his desk, in large part because he was not eager for more keypad-face. But even as he downed the rest of the coffee, he couldn't help but sink down into rehashing how the previous night with Kaity had gone: the good, the bad, and the ugly.

Even if she hadn't specifically meant to hurt him, that was what she'd done. And she'd as much as proven his worst fears: if you cared about someone, they would always leave you. One way or another, everyone left. Gabe almost picked up his phone to text Alex, to apologize for being a bit of an ass. Or maybe he'd even text Kaity, see how she was doing...but he decided against it. She'd already proven that she didn't really need him, and she only wanted him when it was convenient. He had better things to do with his time...or that's what he would tell himself, when the only good thing he could come up with last night was work.

It won't be this way forever, he promised himself. I'll get over her.

Then he turned his laptop back on, hoping that he'd saved his work before passing out practically on top of the damn thing. Luckily he had...but in case the universe couldn't resist giving him one more unpleasant encounter, he heard his phone's text message notification, checked it, and saw that it was from his step-mother. Just great.

Chapter 31

Kaity felt like an intruder, walking into Snapdragon and knowing her days at the studio were limited. She'd almost cut herself off already, opting not to come in tonight or ever again.

She passed by the front desk, where Jenny was seated and taking a call. Smiling brightly, Jenny waved at Kaity, who managed a half-hearted smile and wave back as she walked to her studio.

Everyone was already there, and they didn't pause their preparatory motions as Kaity and Miriam strode in: dancers were pulling on kneepads and legwarmers, rolling out yoga mats, and greeting one another. Sophia said hi to Kaity and Miriam, but Anabelle did not turn to look at them.

Kaity grimly told herself that she just had to get through this class, and the subsequent few weeks until the performance, and then she could be gone for good. Since she'd committed to this performance, she would see it through, feud with Anabelle or no.

"All right, today's technique is a floor jade split, which is in the family of fake splits," Sophia said after warm-up. "Then we'll spend the second hour putting together the pieces in our choreography for the showcase. We have four weeks to go, so those weeks will primarily be rehearsal and polishing up technique."

For the next hour, Kaity was confronted with the grim reality of how inflexible she truly was. It turned out that both Sophia and Jenny had been sneaking in flexibility training to both of their warm-ups, in the form of various lunges and forward folds. But Kaity hadn't been good at those to begin with; even with good alignment in a lunge, she had trouble getting her back leg to fully extend and straighten.

The only good news was that the floor jade was a type of fake split, wherein one started in a plow position or shoulder stand, bent one's legs in towards one's head, grabbed one foot (or ankle, or calf, in Kaity's case), and let the other leg extend long. The body would twist open a bit at the hip, creating the optical illusion that it was a full split or true split, not a twisty one.

Kaity struggled to grab the correct foot with the correct hand; they were supposed to go as opposites, with the right hand grabbing the left foot or vice versa. She found it challenging to let her hips open, exposing her still-slightly-tender crotch to the front mirror, where their imaginary audience was. She didn't know what to do with her free hand, and so it mostly dangled unattractively at her side.

Most of all, Kaity didn't like feeling so...open. Even though she was just in a dimly-lit dance studio with half a dozen mostly-friendly women, she was not a fan of feeling exposed. If Anabelle hadn't pressured her into taking this class, and if she'd known in advance what it would be like, she might not have tried it at all.

"Kaity, are you in pain?" Sophia stooped to her side, concern on her face

Kaity released the leg that was fighting her, took a breath, and answered: "No."

"Okay, just checking. Your face looked either in pain or angry."

With a sigh, Kaity let her whole body melt into the floor. "I'm having a bad day. I'm sorry."

Sophia gently patted Kaity's shoulder. "It's okay. Sometimes we bring our day with us to the studio. I just wanted to make sure nothing was hurting that shouldn't be in this move." She got up and moved on.

Kaity stewed on that. In a way, she was in pain, but it was emotional pain, not physical pain. She didn't know what was happening in her life or what she wanted anymore, as much as she'd been feeling determined to move back to Louisville. And since she'd messed up with Anabelle and with Gabe, maybe she deserved to be hurting. Maybe her day had followed her to the studio, and maybe this was just her life now.

She managed to shake it off and do the remainder of the technique prompts, thankful that there weren't any of the "stare your dance partner in the eyes" exercises this day. Not only did she not want to be paired with Anabelle, she also didn't think she could handle the vulnerability of gazing into someone's soul while in pelvis-baring moves.

The second hour of class marked a transition to the choreography itself, and the tone turned less exploratory and more serious. Sophia had them all sit in a circle, and Kaity was careful to position herself neither next to Anabelle nor directly across from her.

"I know some of you have performed before, while others haven't," Sophia said solemnly, adjusting her glasses. "This choreography is based entirely on movements we've been doing for the past few weeks, so you've been building the confidence you need this entire time. And today we begin putting it together." She played the song again for them, the soft, synth-y cover of "Tainted Love" with a female vocalist that she'd played on day one of the class.

"The six of you will enter from opposite sides of the stage, three on each side, and you will use the melty crawl to approach center stage. Let's practice just that part."

They had to practice the entrance again and again, but as Sophia told them on the run-through she liked best, that entrance ate up nearly thirty seconds, and the cut of the song they were dancing to was only two minutes long. Next, they tacked on a sassy crawl to get the six of them lined up, in a long line from front to back, such that the audience would only really see the first person in the line, with the rest behind them. From there, they pulled back from the crawl into a chest melt, where they did a triceps push-up down to the floor, leaving their butts hanging in the air the longest.

When Sophia was happy with how their entrance looked, she pulled out her phone and filmed them doing it to music. Then everyone clustered around to watch it on their screen. Kaity marveled to herself that they actually looked pretty good, synchronized in their movements. The chest melt had felt like it'd taken an uncomfortably long time, with her ass up in the air just like -

she tried not to think about the previous night - but on camera, it looked just right.

The rest of class flew by as they added in the remaining pieces of the choreography: the bridges with hip circles and the floor jade. Sophia filmed the last run-through, and promised to send it to everyone, so they could rehearse on their own time. She was still deciding on a final pose, she said, but it might involve a simplified version of the partner exercises they'd done, with one person crawling towards another. Kaity cringed to hear that she couldn't just be in her head the whole time, but might have to actually connect with someone. Maybe even Anabelle. But if this was one of the last things she did in Mariontown, she could survive it, no matter how awkward.

"Ready to go?" Miriam asked as she fastened the buckles on her boots. Kaity had practically forgotten that she hadn't driven herself there.

Anabelle had darted out right after class, so Kaity hadn't had to face her. She wondered if another apology was warranted, and then decided to deal with it later.

During the car ride, Miriam played an mp3 of the "Tainted Love" cover, and they talked through the bits of the choreography they understood, and pointed out parts where they needed clarification. It was a fairly companionable way to pass the time, Kaity reflected. Like her, Miriam was not super flexible, and hence did not have pleasant recollections of the splits portion of class.

When Miriam dropped her off, Kaity made sure to thank her for the ride.

"You're welcome," Miriam said. "I hope you fix your issues with Anabelle. I like having dance classes with both of you." Kaity kept smiling even as she turned over that surprising statement in her head. She hadn't really set out to become part of a dance friend group or community, and yet here she was. She definitely hadn't expected Miriam to show up at her doorstep to drag her to class, but that had happened, and it felt...nice?...to be wanted.

Stretching as she let herself into her apartment, Kaity decided that a second bath was definitely warranted, as soon as she put some food in her. Maybe things would be okay eventually after all, even if her apartment still felt too invaded by memories of Gabe. Hopefully he was off somewhere else entertaining himself, done being mad at her as he moved onto the next distraction.

Kaity told herself that it was for the best, though she paused to remember his hands on her body, and told her that it was only natural to want a massage after a day of exertion.

Chapter 32

I'm ready to talk.

The text came two days later, when Kaity was at work, and her inner landscape had smoothed over somewhat. She made the necessary arrangements to take a long lunch, and met Anabelle at a near-east-side tamale place.

They ordered at the counter, then sat in silence. Kaity folded her hands on the table, feeling its smooth surface under her elbows; spring was in full swing, and it was so warm that she had left her cardigan at work, wearing just her cap-sleeve blouse with an A-line skirt.

Finally, Kaity said it. "I'm sorry. I messed up. I get that now."

Anabelle looked down at her own hands, interlaced on the table. Then she spoke.

"I'm not the founder of the divorced ladyfriends group, but I'm an early member. Others have come and gone. Somehow, I found myself in this role of group cheerleader, helping new members find their groove. For women who were freshly divorced, I became something of a divorce doula, helping them through their difficult time."

As Anabelle looked up, Kaity could see that her eyes were moist.

"I love connecting with people. You know me, I'm an extrovert. But so many people treat our group as a temporary friend group until they can find a better fit. I've done my time in therapy; I know I'm not disposable." She smiled weakly. "But it sure as hell felt that way when I learned about your plans."

Kaity unfolded her hands to reach across the table and put her hands over Anabelle's, a comforting gesture momentarily disrupted by the arrival of their food.

"I'm truly sorry, Anabelle. I had no idea. And I wasn't trying to move on from *you* specifically, I just...I don't know. I was convinced I couldn't be happy here since John dragged me here."

Anabelle reached for her fork, and Kaity did the same, eyeing the steaming tamales in front of her: one sweet corn, one green chile chicken.

"Apology accepted," Anabelle said around a mouthful of tamale. "But are you still intent on leaving?"

Kaity shrugged, her mouth full. When she'd chewed and swallowed, appreciating the combination of flavors, she said, "I don't know anymore. I asked my apartment for another two weeks' extension on the decision on my lease. I think you're partly right, that I got lost in my own head about the whole damn situation. My life here is not that bad. It's definitely better since I got divorced."

She paused for another bite. "My job has continued to be decent. Georgia is oddly absent, not looking for reasons to taunt me anymore. I actually really like my time at Snapdragon, and I got sad when I felt like I had to write it off to fulfill my plan to leave." That wasn't entirely the full story; she disliked the vulnerable moments in class recently. But her triceps were looking pretty damn amazing, and she hadn't had any trouble opening jars, a major bonus for a woman living alone.

Anabelle put her fork down. "You know, you're one of the only women in our group to try out some fitness class with me and then stick with it. That's part of why I was surprised when you were going to leave. I thought we'd actually become friends."

"I thought we had too...but I guess I see your point, "Kaity conceded. "Friends don't secretly decide to move away."

Anabelle smiled tremulously. "Friends for sure?"

Kaity smiled back. "For sure." Then she returned to her tamales, feeling good about clearing the air.

After a brief companionable silence, Anabelle said: "So, what about Gabe?"

Kaity sighed. "What about him? I think at this point he was just using me for sex. He got what he wanted—a date to make him look good at his family's Easter, and some practice taking photos with someone who'd never modeled before. We had fun, he helped me remember that I enjoy being flirty and sexy...I think that's all there is to it."

"He hasn't texted or called you?"

"No, which is why I think he's done with me, and never intended much beyond sex in the first place."

Anabelle started to say something, stopped, and started again.

"Do you think...like, he might be hurt too?"

Kaity shook her head. "Unlikely. He was a player before I came along, he'll be fine."

"If you say so. I'm not going to butt in, but it seemed like you were happy spending time with him, and I'll leave it at that."

The conversation turned to other topics, and Kaity returned to work with a bounce in her step. Maybe things weren't perfect in her life, but they were getting better. Maybe she'd stay after all.

The following Monday was the final day of their beginner pole class. Anabelle ambushed Kaity as she was getting out of her car. "You ready to perform? Did you bring anyone?"

Kaity shouldered her workout bag and sigh. "I completely forgot that we could bring a guest."

"Don't worry, I didn't take initiative and invite Gabe, though trust me, I thought about it as a way to get your two to make up." Kaity was grateful that Anabelle reined herself in for once.

As they walked into Snapdragon, there were only two men sitting in the waiting room, talking with one another in Spanish. Andrea's husband and Maricela's boyfriend were waiting until they were invited in. Jenny ran everyone through warm-ups, and then they ran their beginner pole routine twice before getting ready to perform it one at a time for each other. Since Andrea and Maricela had guests, they were the first two to go. Following Jenny's lead, all the other dance students were loudly enthusiastic during each routine, clapping and shouting encouragement.

Anabelle went next, and then Lin and her friends. Miriam went after that, having chosen a bass-intensive industrial song. Kaity went last, after telling Jenny the title and artist of her song. She'd opted for a slightly obscure jazz song, but as she went through the moves of their little routine, she was happy with her choice. She nailed the slinky and pole sit, though her fireman's spin was a little rough. When she put her back to the pole, walked her feet out, and then slid down to take her final pose, she was breathing heavily and feeling her heart beating rapidly. If this was what performing was like, even if just for a small audience of classmates, she was glad that she had another two weeks to prepare for the Snapdragon showcase, where she and the others would be dancing to Sophia's slinky choreography.

"Nice job!" Anabelle squealed, bounding over to hug Kaity once she got up from her pose. Miriam handed over Kaity's phone, since she'd been the one filming it, and she said, "Well done." And Kaity glowed in the praise of her friends.

The work party arrived sooner than Kaity had thought it would.

She had agreed to go to a weekly conditioning class with both Anabelle and Miriam, in addition to continuing with their beginner class as it advanced to the next level. Anabelle had suggested it after their pole class hesitantly, as though she knew she was always the one initiating activities, and her friends might depart once they found their own will to thrive again. But Kaity had enthusiastically agreed, and so had Miriam, to their surprise (she had muttered something about not wanting to just be a skinny goth girl anymore).

Even though the time passed quickly, Kaity had still hoped to have a date on her arm. She had thought about texting Gabe. But neither thing had happened, and Kaity was resigned to going alone.

Her company had rented out the dolphin pavilion of the Mariontown Zoo, which was exciting to Kaity because she hadn't yet made it to the zoo.

As she pulled up to park, she made a note to invite Anabelle to the zoo next time they had a free weekend, which would likely be after the showcase. Saturdays and Sundays were now spent stretching on someone's living room floor or running different outfits through the wringer.

Kaity took a deep breath before getting out of her car. She knew Georgia would be there. Possibly even with John as a plus-one, since employees were encouraged to bring family members to events if they didn't have a partner they wanted to bring.

She took another deep breath, then smoothed her hands over her skirt. Her muscle-to-fat ratio has been shifting ever so slightly; another person might not notice, but Kaity did, and she liked it. She'd chosen to wear a pencil skirt John had always said made her look fat, but after getting both Anabelle and Miriam's opinion on it, she decided that it accentuated her curves in a good way, hinting at the muscle while showing off the sexy roundness.

One more deep breath. She could do this.

A knuckle rapped at her car window.

Kaity jolted in her seat, then turned to see who it was.

It was Gabe. And he had flowers.

Chapter 33

G abe peered in at Kaity's shocked face and hoped
that she wouldn't just tell him off.

After a moment, she collected herself, opened the car
door, and got out. He admired the outfit she'd chosen,
which highlighted her curves in delectable ways. Before
she could talk, he thrust the flowers at her. She accepted
them, as though it were an automatic reflex and not
exactly what she wanted to do.

"I was an ass and I'm sorry," he said in a rush.

She paused, a wary look on her face.

"I agreed to come with you to your work party, and
I want to hold up my end of the bargain. Especially
because my step-mom got in touch and invited me to
my sister's middle school graduation. I think that happened in large part because of you. Because you were
a good influence on me, even back then." Gabe had
mulled this last part over, and come to the conclusion
that he could've tried to smooth things over by asking
Kaity to be his fake girlfriend at all his family events,
which would've been a win for his family life, but a loss
for his personal life. He also didn't want to sound too

mercenary; while he'd rehearsed this talk with Alex, she had pointed out the pitfalls there.

In the mulling-over process, Gabe had realized that not only had Kaity improved his general life quality, she had also inspired him to improve his own life. To let people in. To not be afraid of the pain of loss.

Kaity was still just looking at the flowers, not even making eye contact with him. Clearly, he had to keep talking. And do better in the future.

"I...shouldn't have said those things," he said softly. "You deserve better. And, maybe I'm not what you want, but please let me be your arm candy tonight."

Kaity finally raised her eyes to his. He felt the start of longing in his body. But he also felt saddened by the sorrow in her eyes, the serious cast to them.

"I should probably apologize too," she said. "I didn't want you to feel...discarded. Like I was leaving. I don't think I'm leaving, by the way. But I didn't know how to tell you."

Gabe smiled hesitantly. She smiled back.

Then she looked down at the bouquet. "I think I'd feel weird bringing flowers to a work function...is it okay to leave this in my car?"

"I brought them for you, so you can do whatever you want with them," Gabe replied. Then he got a better idea.

He reached down to pluck one of the flowers out of the bouquet—a red carnation—and then tucked it into Kaity's hair, which she was alluringly wearing down. While there, he lingered, and let his fingertips drift across her cheek. She blushed.

He wasn't imagining it; there was still a connection between them. After he'd had that agonizing all-nighter, after he'd gotten the text from his step-mom, after he'd apologized to Alex over a beer...he'd realized that Kaity had not intended to set off his abandonment issues (which was Alex's favorite way to sum up all his problems). Further, he'd realized—and told Alex, who made grossed-out gagging noises—that Kaity was the only woman he'd ever dated (technically, fake-dated) who'd noticed which beers he liked, and had made a specific point of surprising him with them the last time they got together. She hadn't just been using him to get high-quality modeling photos for a portfolio, like other women in his past. She had been thoughtful and caring throughout. And now, Kaity, for all their misunderstandings, still seemed to want him.

And he still wanted her, even if he had fuck-all idea about what to do about it.

Kaity stashed the flowers in her car and strode towards the dolphin pavilion, Gabe's arm linked with hers. She wasn't completely sure how she felt about him...but if the rest of her life was any indication, starting to pay attention to the good things right in front of her face was probably a good move.

"Wait," she said, an unpleasant thought brewing in her mind. "How did you find out where exactly this was going to be?" She did not want to find out that she'd been sleeping with someone with stalker tendencies.

"Oh, that...someone Alex works with is friends with someone that Anabelle works with. I told you Marion-town was socially a small town."

Kaity mulled that over. If this was the smallest amount of interference that Anabelle could manage, that was acceptable.

They found the entrance to the dolphin pavilion, and Kaity took a moment to appreciate the way the building was constructed, with eye-level windows into the tanks throughout. Dolphins frolicked in framed views of the water, twisting gracefully around the passageways lining the main room, which was filled with tables and the chairs orbiting them.

Gabe leaned down to whisper in Kaity's ear, and the tickle of his breath gave her shivers. She told herself that it was because it was chilly inside the pavilion.

"Remind me again, who are the important people to know?"

She whispered back: "Antonio is my boss, you'll definitely meet him. Georgia is my ex-sister-in-law who doesn't like me. Liam and Breanna are the two coders I work with most closely on my educational modules."

He put his arm around her shoulders and whispered back, "I can handle that much."

They were on the early side; the doors opened at 6:30, dinner was served at 7, and it was 6:35. Kaity spotted Antonio and made her way over, making sure to introduce Gabe as her boyfriend. Antonio's eyes lit up; Kaity assumed he was happy that she'd found someone. As more people were arriving, Antonio excused himself to go greet them.

The open bar was on the far side of the room. They both seemed to notice it at the same time.

"Care for a drink?" Gabe asked.

"I'll wait to have a glass of wine with dinner. But I'll take something sparkling and nonalcoholic for now."

"I'll go grab it for you, then."

Left on her own, Kaity slowly spun around, taking in the aquatic surroundings. She spotted Liam on his way over to the bar and chatted for a few minutes. When Liam continued his trajectory, Kaity continued to look around, and saw that there were a few passageways leading to other cavernous enclosures with yet more glimpses of the water. Slowly, more people walked into the main room, either to visit the bar or to start claiming seats on the understanding that it would be open seating.

Kaity figured she could pick a seat and Gabe would find her. She turned away from the bar, scanning the tables, which all had colorful floral centerpieces.

That's when she heard her ex-husband John saying her name.

Gabe was carrying a local pilsner in one hand and a mocktail in the other when he saw someone talking to Kaity...and it was as if that someone made her shrink, made her curl into herself and become physically smaller. He hurried his pace, trying not to spill the drinks.

"Kaity?" the man was saying. "How have you been? Looks like you finally lost some weight."

She looked so miserable, cringing while opening her mouth to respond, that Gabe stepped it up and arrived just in time to slide an arm around her shoulders and interrupt.

"Hi. I'm Gabe. Kaity's date. And yes, I agree she looks wonderful."

The man—who must be John—shot him a baleful glance. Gabe took his appearance in, noting the scraggly beard, slender frame, and sandy hair pulled back in a low ponytail. Being an artist himself, Gabe was not one to be the manhood police when it came to men having long hair or not, but John's mildly unkempt appearance set off a reaction of distaste in him. He tightened his arm around Kaity. She looked up at him gratefully.

"Let's go find some seats," Gabe suggested to Kaity. He steered her away, casting glances behind to make sure John didn't follow them; instead, John went to the bar. Then when they were away enough, Gabe apologized for steering her.

"No, it's okay," she said, seated and sipping on her drink. "I froze up."

Gabe waited until she'd put down the drink, and took her hands in his. "Hey, I'm here to be your shield if you need me. You'd said he was a jerk, but I didn't think he was *that* much of a jerk. God, who says that stuff?"

She smiled wanly. Gabe was just happy to see her smile. "Well, my ex does, apparently. You should have heard some of the stuff he said while we were married." The thought of someone verbally abusing Kaity, let alone for completely bullshit reasons like how her body looked, made Gabe's jaw clench.

Kaity stiffened up again, looking over his shoulder.

"Oh no, there's Georgia."

Gabe swiveled his head and beheld a young woman with blond hair swirling around her shoulders walking towards them, a smirk twisting her red lips. He could practically feel the tension radiating off of Kaity next to him.

But then something caught her attention before she could reach their table: John was shaking hands with someone near the bar, and loudly introducing himself as Georgia's brother, and the ex-husband of Kaity, the fat overpaid one who—

Georgia whipped around and went to intercept him. Gabe and Kaity watched as Georgia berated her brother for already being drunk, and as John belligerently talked back, and as Georgia got them both out of the main room before things escalated.

"Well, that happened," Kaity said when they turned back to face each other. Gabe could only nod and take a sip of his beer, not entirely sure what he had witnessed other than that it had been bad and getting worse.

"I don't want to be mean," Kaity continued, causing Gabe to arch his eyebrows, "but I think they deserve each other. I can only assume John badgered his sister into being her plus-one, and she accepted without realizing what a shitshow it would be."

"Sounds about right," Gabe said. Kaity didn't curse very often, so hearing her say "shitshow" was amusing, but it also gestured at the severity of the situation. He imagined his stepmother would fit in well with that level of nastiness, but then again, she seemed to be giving him a chance lately, so maybe he should give her a chance.

"Dumpster fire aside," he said, putting his arm around Kaity again, "not a bad start to the night." That got a laugh out of her, which was music to Gabe's ears. If he hadn't been sure that he was into Kaity before, now he was. How anyone could look at her and not see that she was amazing was beyond him. She was smart, organized, down-to-earth, beautiful, and giving. Most of the women he'd dated nabbed one or two traits on that list at most. If John tried to reenter the main room, Gabe wasn't sure that he could keep himself from telling him off or worse, because Kaity only deserved the best.

Whether Gabe counted as good enough for Kaity, or someone she'd even want...that was a separate question entirely. Gabe tried to put it out of his mind and just enjoy the evening as arm candy.

Chapter 34

T hree courses and one glass of wine later, Kaity was full, both with food and with schmoozing. The important speeches had been made, hard-working employees had been thanked, and thus she figured it was a good time to get out of there. The important thing was, they weren't the first people to leave.

Technically, John had been the first to leave; when Georgia had returned without him, but with a barely-repressed scowl on her face, Kaity imagined that she must've stuffed her brother into a cab home. For a moment, she felt sorry for Georgia. She, too, had had to deal with John's alcohol-exacerbated tempers while in close quarters. And there'd been no one to take her side or defend her.

Kaity leaned over and whispered to Gabe after the programming had ended, "Are you ready to leave?"

He bent his head close to hers to hear her over the susurrating crowd, and Kaity liked that he had leaned in to hear her. To pay attention to her. To be closer to her. They might have started with a fake relationship, but this didn't feel fake. He said something affirmative, and then they were up and walking, his arm around her shoulders, saying their goodbyes. The embrace of his arm felt natural and easy.

Gabe walked Kaity to her car, and for a moment she'd almost forgotten that they'd driven separately.

She stood with her back to her car, remembering their first fake-date over a month ago, which had ended much like this.

This time, she wasn't sure if she wanted it to end. But she also didn't want to move too quickly, to pave over recent wounds. After all, she'd moved quickly, on autopilot, when she'd decided that returning to Louisville was undoubtedly her best option.

So Kaity raised her hands and put them on Gabe's chest, holding their bodies a few inches apart. She looked up into his warm brown eyes. And she said: "I'll let you know when I'm ready."

His face showed surprise and disappointment, but to his credit, he nodded, leaned in for a light hug, and then backed away.

Kaity climbed into her car, feeling proud of herself for setting a boundary, but also a little shaken. Taking Gabe home would have been very, very enjoyable. But she didn't want to do it because they'd been on one more fake date; she wanted to do it for real.

The rest of her evening, she anticipated while starting her car, would include a bath and some time with her vibrator. Hopefully she'd also get some ideas as to how to get her life together, if it were actually possible to have her cake and eat it too.

Kaity spent the rest of the weekend being a homebody, with the exception of one workout class at Snapdragon with Anabelle. She reorganized her loose-leaf tea collection, did laundry and a bit of meal prep, and hung more art on her walls. It was the kind of quiet life she enjoyed, and she wanted to give herself permission to sink into it fully before deciding if she wanted to share it with someone.

On reflection, the quiet moments made her happy. But sometimes they dragged on, and the prospect of yet another cup of herbal tea while reading felt a bit hollow. She thought about texting Gabe, because doubtless he was up to something exciting or artistic or both...but she made herself wait. She wanted to be certain that she was comfortable in her solitude before she invited someone in for real.

Monday morning saw Kaity at the office early, planning for a series of back-to-back meetings with an extra travel mug of tea for an energy boost midway through. She also wore another pencil skirt, a new purchase with Anabelle's approval, for a confidence boost. As Anabelle had said, there was no sense in hiding her body or pretending she had a different one than she actually did, so there was no reason not to wear curve-hugging clothing.

As usual, she performed well in the first few meetings, and then she got a break for lunch before the next few. This was the time of year when most universities wanted their employees to take new trainings on identifying phishing scams, so she had security on the brain. She popped into the break room to retrieve and heat up the stir fry she'd stuck in the fridge earlier in the day.

Georgia was there. For once, she didn't look at Kaity with active malice in her eyes.

"Hey, do you have a minute?" she asked.

Kaity continued what she was doing, getting the snap top off the container so she could put it in the microwave. Once it was heating up, she turned to where Georgia was standing. Kaity nodded to answer the question, observing how Georgia stood with her arms crossed in front of her chest, slightly hunching in a way that did not make her look happy.

"You saw what a wreck my brother was," Georgia said, still holding herself stiffly. "It's been bad for a while. When you two first moved back here, I hoped that we could all be close. He made it sound like you were the one keeping him from his family, and then it was your fault that the divorce happened."

Kaity remained silent and simply raised her eyebrows.

"He's my brother, of course I took his side. After, he got suspicious of you and your reasoning, and he thought you were hiding things from him. Money, an affair, whatever. It's part of why I took the job here, because he kept pestering me to find out what your paycheck was. So, I'm sorry for that. If you got a nastygram from his attorney, that's on me."

Kaity took a calming breath, or what she hoped was a calming breath. That situation was handled by now, but it'd still been incredibly stressful.

"You've met our parents," Georgia continued. Kaity had. She had not gotten along too well with them, and John had repeatedly reassured her that it wasn't their fault, they were highly judgmental and image-focused when it came to everyone and everything. "They wanted

John to save face and maintain his appearance of being in the right, so it became this whole thing to massage his ego and make him feel like he'd been cheated or wronged by you."

"That's ridiculous," Kaity couldn't help from blurting out. The microwave beeped at the same time, and she turned away to retrieve her food.

"Yeah, well, it just got worse," Georgia said. "The rants were nonstop. You saw how he was with the drinking. I only agreed to bring him to the work party because he promised he'd cleaned up his act. And worse, he lost the place he was renting. When you left, I guess you were the one doing all the bills, and he never picked up the slack."

"I see," said Kaity. She hadn't really been expecting any of this, and she wasn't sure how she felt about it. "Um, I have another meeting coming up, is that what you wanted to tell me?"

Georgia smiled bitterly. "Just that I'm sorry. You were always decent to me here, and you had no reason to be. I'll be requesting a transfer to another office, since John is moving back in with our parents, where I'm currently living. If my family wants to keep being toxic, they can do it without me." Then she strode out of the room, leaving Kaity standing next to the microwave, her stir fry and brown rice releasing steam into the air in whorls. Kaity held a hand over the steam, and felt it warm her fingers. Life was weird sometimes.

Chapter 35

I t was the first night of their new beginner pole class, and Kaity was still reeling from the conversation with Georgia, which she'd had to put out of her mind in order to get through her remaining meetings. Driving up to Snapdragon, though, she replayed it in her head, and felt...not quite closure, but something close to it.

Kaity didn't think she wished John ill, but she felt vindicated in one area: he had berated her for being detail-oriented and anxious, and for caring about things he deemed illogical and stupid. At the same time, her careful attention to small matters like budgeting and records and bills had ensured that they were able to live comfortably while together. She'd grown so used to him talking down to her that she'd forgotten about her strengths. She was plenty strong on her own, and her meticulous habits were not something to mock.

As she put her car in park, another puzzle piece fell into place: John must have already been encountering financial difficulties when he sent Georgia after her. He could be charismatic when he wanted to—it was part of why she'd initially been drawn to him—so if he were tru- ly convinced that Kaity had wronged him by withholding something important, it was no wonder he'd gotten Georgia and his attorney on his side to investigate. At least Georgia had eventually seen through the bullshit.

Kaity opened her car door and stood, noting that her thighs had only stuck to the car seat a little in the sunny weather. She'd started coming to pole class just in shorts if the weather was warm enough, since she no longer felt like she needed to cover up out of shame.

She turned towards the studio, only to shriek as Anabelle manifested in front of her.

"Oh my god!" Kaity gasped. "I didn't see you."

"I was in stealth mode," Anabelle smirked. Indeed, she was in black shorts and a black sports bra, a bit more somber than her usual color palette. "I'm ready to train hard, how about you?" Kaity had to admit that she'd been feeling a little panicky about learning new, undoubtedly harder things, but she gave Anabelle a thumbs-up in an attempt to fake it until she made it.

Jenny switched up the warm-up for their new session, and as Kaity huffed and puffed through a series of Zumba-like dance movies, she wondered if every time a new thing came into her life it would feel sucky at first but eventually feel okay.

Then it was time to learn their new moves. Standing with one side to her pole, Jenny hooked a knee around it...and used that to climb up the pole, with her other leg folding in to act as a support.

"This is called a side climb," Jenny explained. "Everyone stand with one side to the pole, let's make it our right sides so I can give instructions for everyone using the same descriptions." From there, it grew insanely hard from Kaity's perspective, and she was pretty sure the top of each foot was going to be bruised after they'd tried it on each side. But she left the studio with a smile on her face, and after briefly conferring with Anabelle and Miriam, she decided to continue the strength-training classes with them, so they could all level up together faster.

The three of them went out to dinner to celebrate, opting to go to a brewery one plaza down the road...and while there, Kaity decided that she was ready to see Gabe again. She asked to try tasters of a few different beers while they were deciding on appetizers to share, and she then made mental notes about which beers to bring home, working with what she knew of Gabe's preferences to guess which he'd enjoy. The house sour hadn't really been on her radar as something she would enjoy...but it was, and she did, so she opted for a glass with her meal.

Then she sent him a text: *I'm ready. Want to ask me out for a date?*

It felt like a bold move, but with the post-pole high, she felt good about it. Surely it helped that Anabelle and Miriam were cheering her on, too.

The response from Gabe came in by the time their food had arrived: *Yes. Tomorrow night? I'll pick you up.*

Kaity answered in the affirmative, and then enjoyed the remainder of her meal with her friends. They started with spinach artichoke dip and the whipped feta and honey, and then Kaity had a Nashville hot chicken sandwich. Not quite as good as the ones in Louisville from her favorite restaurant there, but it was a passable substitute...and the company she was in made everything better.

Chapter 36

T he next day at work dragged for Kaity, even though not having to look over her shoulder for Georgia coming at her, claws out, also made her time in the office feel a little less stressful. She'd worn a cute floral dress to the office, one that was flattering yet still modest, so once she got home a little after 5pm, she changed into something a little slinkier. The charcoal gray dress Anabelle had helped her pick out was crushed velvet with a deep V-neck, and it hugged her curves.

Gabe picked her up around 6pm, and he told her that the destination was a surprise. Kaity could tell that they were driving south, and then they were on Mass Ave, pulling around to park near a restaurant she'd heard of but hadn't yet visited, Union 60.

After parking, Gabe got out and opened Kaity's door for her, then offered her his arm to walk in to the restaurant. Gabe opened the large glass door for her, and then offered his arm again. Walking in with him, Kaity felt profoundly lucky to have someone who was not just hot, but also really kind, escorting her in. And she got the impression that he felt the same way, that he was proud to show her off but also happy simply that it was her accompanying him.

Kaity looked over the menu, and consulted Gabe on what was good there. They opted to share the duck fat and rosemary fries, along with a beet and bleu cheese salad, at least for their appetizers. Kaity ordered a cactus pear cocktail, and Gabe got the Chilly Agua blood orange IPA.

"I was tempted to surprise you with something," Gabe said, getting her attention as she was looking around the large, glass-backed bar, "but I get the impression that you dislike surprises." She smiled wryly in response; that was pretty spot-on. Gabe got out his phone and unlocked it to show her a picture of a large, framed photo...of her.

"This is one of the prints from the shoot we did a few weeks ago. I got it printed and framed, and I'm planning to show it at a gallery. But I wanted to check with you first."

It was one of the photos where Kaity was on her back, her head tilted to one side, her hair cascading around her shoulders. One hand curled gently in on itself, as though the fingers were yearning to touch the palm, but not quite brave enough. The overall feeling of the piece was dreamy and sensual. Kaity felt herself blushing, to see herself reflected like this through an artist's gaze...an artist who was also, perhaps, becoming her lover.

"I'm..." she paused. "I never thought I'd see myself like this. But when I'm with you, this is how I feel."

Gabe leaned into take her hands across the table. His skin was warm, and Kaity's heart quickened.

The waitress arrived right then with their appetizers, and they broke apart. Kaity took another sip of her cocktail to hide her awkward flush.

Reaching for some duck fat fries, Gabe said: "So, can I try to show these photos of you, if I find a fitting gallery?"

Kaity had just loaded some salad into her mouth, so she nodded. Once she was done chewing, she said: "Yes, for sure. I'm still just, like, really flattered." She reached for some fries next. The duck fat coated her tongue with a delicious, savory flavor. She went for more.

"I'm glad you're in," Gabe said. "I've got a spot in mind."

"Oh?" Kaity managed to say, around a mouthful of fries. She finished chewing, savoring the flavors, and washed it all down with a sip of her cocktail.

"Now *that* part will be a surprise. But I think you'll like it," Gabe said. Kaity faked a pout, but ended up smiling around the edges of it.

"Did I tell you what happened at work yesterday?" she asked. Between preparing for her new series class at Snapdragon, and getting ready for tonight's occasion, she hadn't had a lot of time to casually text Gabe. When he shook his head, sending his brown curls bouncing, she filled him in on the end of the drama with Georgia and John. He listened, asked a few clarifying questions, and then fell silent as their entrees arrived: they'd decided to share the shrimp and grits, along with the duck confit. Kaity switched to a white wine, the house sauvignon blanc, while Gabe continued to sip on his beer.

Even as they enjoyed their meal, Kaity could feel Gabe's eyes on her. When he reached across the table to grab a forkful of the plate that had landed nearer her, his hand usually brushed up against hers. His knee found hers under the table frequently, in a way that she could tell was intentional. Kaity filled up with warmth at all the little gestures, so different than her marriage where the only expected touch was sexual in nature.

When they'd finished most of what was on the plates before them, Gabe reached over to touch Kaity before their server could return and ask if they wanted dessert. "If you like, we can get dessert here, but I picked up some truffles from M-town's Best Chocolate, and I thought we could enjoy them back at your place."

Feeling Gabe's warm hand on hers, Kaity took stock. She was feeling pleasantly full, her taste buds satiated, and the rest of her...definitely not full. Nowhere near it.

She batted her eyelashes, and murmured: "I'm in." Simultaneously, she wondered where this coquettish version of her had come from. Anabelle would be proud. It was like she and Gabe were taking turns setting the tone...and feeling like she could share these moments with someone was novel and sexy. She liked being in control because she liked knowing that she'd be okay at the end of the day, but being able to trust someone else to take the reins was an alluring possibility.

Gabe signaled that he was ready for the check, paid it, and then escorted Kaity back to his car. He drove back to her place with one hand on her thigh the whole time, leaving Kaity awash in a haze of desires piqued but not yet satisfied.

When they reached her place, Gabe turned to her. "Do you want me to come in?"

Impulsively, she leaned over to kiss him, just a quick peck on the lips. "You said there'd be chocolate, so yes. More than that, and we'll have to see." She meant it as an invitation, and it looked like Gabe took it as such, given the speed with which he bolted from the car and opened her door, pausing to retrieve a small bag, in order to escort her inside.

His hand strayed from the middle of her back to lower, and lower, which Kaity took to be a very good sign indeed. After a sensuous dinner, she was ready for more. And Gabe looked like he was too, judging from his eager caresses as she dug her keys from her purse and unlocked her door.

She couldn't help but think about the last time he'd been over, when they'd had mind-blowing sex but then been torn apart by the revelation that she was probably going to move. A niggling anxious thought that this could turn out to be a repeat surfaced in Kaity's mind, but she did her best to stifle it. She wasn't sure where it was coming from, but it seemed likely that the recent run-in with her ex had caused all sorts of unpleasant things to resurface for her, because of the time she'd spent in the habit of making herself smaller so as not to irk her ex.

Those days were behind her now.

Kaity reached to grab Gabe's hand, and tugged him into her apartment, her thoughts ablaze.

Chapter 37

G abe let Kaity guide him into her place. He paused for a moment to look around, noticing that she'd put a few more homey touches around on the walls and shelves: a framed photo of her, Anabelle, and Miriam making faces at a restaurant adorned one bookshelf, while a Snapdragon logo magnet was on her fridge. Those little touches made it look less and less likely that she was going to leave, which put Gabe more at ease.

It had seemed that she wanted to be courted, so he'd played the role with joy and panache. Hopefully his efforts had paid off, not just in the sense that ideally sex would follow, but also in the sense that this was a game he could easily and happily play for a very long time. Kaity was special, and she deserved to be treated as such.

When she pulled out some local brews to pair with the chocolates, that simply cemented Gabe's attraction to her. They sat at her small dining room table, and Kaity made small noises of delight when he unboxed the chocolates: two dark chocolate salted caramels, one raspberry truffle, and one persimmon truffle. Gabe insisted that she try each one first, and she did, biting in and eating roughly half before offering it to Gabe. Their fingers grew sticky, and Gabe made a show out of licking Kaity's fingers clean, causing her to giggle.

By the time they'd made it through the chocolate and a few sips of the beer, Gabe noticed the conversation slowing, and the amount that they touched each other increasing. He checked one hand for chocolate, then deliberately put it on her thigh and slid up, the soft texture of the velvet tickling his palm. Kaity shivered, holding his gaze, and then stood.

"Join me in bed?" she said.

"Certainly," he replied, feeling his heartbeat pick up.

He followed her into her bedroom. She stood with her back to him, arms held out, and he took the hint and figured out how to lift her dress over her head. He stayed behind her, planting kisses on her shoulders. Already, she was beginning to moan and sway a little under his touch, so he used one hand to gather and pull her hair out of the way, going for a firm but not painful grip. That freed up the back of her neck, so he kissed her there as well, slipping in little hints of teeth, which made her jerk under his mouth. With his other hand, he caressed her breasts through her bra, then teased lower and traced fingertips over her underwear.

"Mmm," Kaity said, and then backed up so that her ass was rubbing against him, making his pants seem tighter than they had been before.

Gabe kept kissing her neck, then let go of her hair, not minding when it piled up against his face. He used both hands to find where her bra latched and undo it, and then he slid down her panties. Exposed, Kaity swayed, and Gabe stepped back to look at her.

"You're beautiful," he said. She blushed, but didn't duck down her head, as though she'd kicked out some of the shyness in the last few weeks.

He guided her to the edge of the bed, and paused to pull down the sheets. Then he had her recline on the bed. He wanted her...but he also wanted to tease her just a little, to flirt and take up the heat a bit. He shucked his own pants and shirt, then knelt by the bed. She looked at him expectantly, so he leaned in to kiss her. She writhed a little, and Gabe felt himself hardening even more.

He broke off the kiss and reached down the bed for just the top sheet. He drew it up to Kaity's chin, and watched as she looked at him quizzically, her lovely features going from pliant arousal to curiosity.

Leaning down to whisper in her ear, he started to touch her body through the sheet. "I've been thinking about you since you texted me. The things I wanted to do to you." He felt her shudder lightly under the sheet. "I've been thinking about teasing you, making you beg for it." He paused around one nipple, circling it with his fingers. Her back arched. He nibbled at her ear before continuing. "But that means teasing myself too, and I don't know how much longer I can be patient for." He drew the sheet down to her stomach, making sure it grazed her nipples, which he could now see were hard. He began kissing from her ear down her neck down to her breasts, and he feasted while she squirmed under his touch. With one hand, he pressed the sheet into her pubic area, giving her something to grind against, since he'd noticed her hips beginning to work. With her other hand, he reached down and freed himself from his boxers, lightly stroking himself.

"Gabe," she moaned.

He stopped kissing her breasts. "Yes? Is there something you want?"

She reached for his head with both hands, drawing his face to hers for a deep kiss. "I want you. Now."

That was what he'd longed to hear, that she wanted him, and it wasn't just a reaction to a bad day or a fling before she planned to leave town. He continued to kiss Kaity, and then pushed the sheet off her and climbed onto the bed with her, taking his boxers the rest of the way off while en route.

Laying half atop her, he took one more teasing shot: "*How* do you want me?"

Kaity lifted her head off the pillow in obvious frustration. "I want you in me, you cad!"

He chuckled, and slid off her to retrieve a condom from his pants pockets on the floor. Then he returned to the bed, letting his body not quite overlap with hers, so that he could sneak some fingers downward to begin playing with her clit. Based on the noises she was making and the grind of her hips, it felt good. He worked a finger inside her, then a second.

"You're so wet," he whispered in her ear, feeling her answering shudder. "And you're so hot." Her hips began to lift off the bed, so eager to work into his fingers. He suspected that no one had ever really talked dirty to her before, and he made a mental note to play with her with words even more.

He withdrew his hand to use both hands to get the condom out of the package and on, and then he overlaid his body with hers, finding her entrance and pushing in. Kaity moaned and tucked her hips to welcome him deeper, it seemed, and then Gabe was blissfully fucking her. He buried his head in her neck as he lost himself in the strokes. Her fingernails scored his back, making him fuck her harder. He wanted to fuck her until he came, but he knew it might not get her off, so he slowed his pace, grabbed around her hips, and rolled onto his back, managing to stay inside her the whole time.

"Ride me," he said, as he watched her get oriented and wipe her hair from her face. She looked good on top of him, her breasts bouncing slightly with each movement, and her hips and thigh engulfing his lower half. Kaity began to fuck him, and he put his hands on her waist just to have a reason to touch her. It didn't look like she was getting closer to climaxing, though, so he grabbed one of her hands and guided it to her clit.

"I want you to touch yourself," and he watched understanding fill her eyes. Kaity continued to bounce on top of him, but the rhythm changed slightly, and she hunched over more, as her right hand went to town while her left hand braced against his chest. Her moans picked up urgency, and then she was gasping and jerking on top of him. Gabe felt her vaginal muscles clench around him, and that was almost enough to take him over the edge. He moved his hands down to her hips, and used that placement to keep her pumping up and down, trusting that she would say something if it were too much.

But Kaity looked lost in sensation, her eyes half-lidded and her mouth falling open as she continued to gasp with each stroke as he guided her hips atop his. It was so hot, knowing that she'd just come and she was taking more, that Gabe came soon after, spasming into her. He held her hips still while his body resounded with the orgasm, and then he let her slide off and down and curl up into his arms.

He kissed her wherever he could reach her, and held her, and felt extremely glad that she'd reached out to let him take her on a date. He could get used to this.

Chapter 38

Kaity stayed blissfully rolled up in Gabe's arms until she realized that she had to pee. Excusing herself to use the bathroom felt a whole lot less awkward than the first time when they'd had sex.

She came back and nestled in for more attention, which he obligingly gave, playing with her hair and stroking her arms and waist.

"That was fun," she whispered to him.

"Agreed," he said. "We should do it again sometime."

"Are we going out for real now?" she asked. She paused, trying to ditch the hesitation and added, "because I'd like to."

He kissed the top of her head. "I'm in if you are. Just..." and his voice grew soft, and small, "don't leave me like you almost did."

Kaity wiggled deeper into his arms. "Deal. Don't make me regret caring about you to the extent that I do."

"Done."

She felt her breathing slow, and his too. That observation prodded her to wakefulness. "Are you spending the night? Is this our first overnight?"

"I can if you want me to," Gabe said. "I'm fine to take this slow."

"I think I'd like that," Kaity replied. There was a time when she'd only wanted her own space, and she'd wanted it to be perfect for her. Now she thought it might be nice to share her space from time to time with the right person.

Her mind raced ahead to brushing her teeth and pulling out a spare package of toothbrushes so Gabe could use one. Would she let him have a drawer eventually? Then something else occurred to her.

"The showcase is in two weeks, oh my god!"

"What about it? I'll be there photographing."

"Won't it be, like, awkward if we're together?"

Gabe drew himself up on one elbow so he could lock eyes with Kaity. "Unlike your piece of shit ex, I'm proud to be with you. Tell the whole world for all I care. I'm here with you now. I'll be there with you then. I do, of course, have to take pictures of other women who are sometimes scantily clad, but you're the only scantily-clad woman I will interact with on any physical basis."

Kaity leaned in for a kiss. And then another. This, she decided, was quite doable. Gabe was quite a catch...and he was *hers*.

Kaity spent the two weeks prior to the summer showcase frantically texting Anabelle and Miriam to schedule practice dates outside of class. They all had the routine memorized by then, so it was just a matter of making sure the details were perfect: a hair toss here, a booty twerk there. Kaity wore out one pair of kneepads and bought another, and she wasn't the only one.

The day before the showcase, they held a dress rehearsal at Snapdragon, and that was when Gabe photographed every routine.

Kaity felt as nervous as though she were performing for an actual audience, not just one photographer and then a handful of other pole dancers who'd congregated to watch this particular set. She squeezed Anabelle's and Miriam's hands during the pep talk Sophia gave them about pairing each motion with a mood and making sure they took moments to really be in their bodies, feeling as sensual as possible.

With the lights dimmed as they would be in the showcase, Kaity and the five other dancers took their positions, just outside the official space of the stage...not that it was raised, Kaity had a moment to reflect on gratefully.

When the characteristic double-beat of the bass of the "Tainted Love" cover began, Kaity, Nina, and Miriam melty-crawled from their side of the stage towards the other three dancers. They swayed their hips from side to side in time with the music, and when they reached the center stage, slotting in with every other dancer facing the opposite direction, they all lowered their chests, leaving their butts in the air for a moment. Then, with another double-beat bass thump, they dropped their hips to the floor and up again. With the lyrics came a direction change, so that the six dancers had their heads almost touching while their legs pointed outward like the hands of a clock. They all pushed up into bridges and gyrated their hips, once again catching the double-beat bass thump to grind their hips towards the ground. Another change of their formation, and they were sassy-crawling away from one another, only to do knee spins back to face each other and drop to the ground on their bellies, then sensually roll onto their backs to do bridges, then shoulder stands with fancy leg swings, then the floor jade splits.

As the song came to a crescendo, the six dancers paired off, and Kaity crawled over to Anabelle, practically crawling over her while Anabelle slid away underneath her. Kaity did the circular cat-and-cow motion, letting her hair whip in circles to the beat of the music. As the crescendo faded, the dancers all crawled off stage, like unsatisfied succubi searching for new targets.

They then stood, linked hands, and went back to the stage for their bow, as Sophia had instructed them to do. Kaity's heart felt like it was beating a million miles a minute, and she gasped for breath, wondering why anyone would do this to themselves on purpose. Anabelle and Miriam jumped up and down and hugged each other, and the other three dancers—Nina, Leanne, and Jo—gave each other high fives. Clearly this was not their first rodeo.

Hands hugged her from behind, and Kaity leaned into Gabe's warmth. "You were amazing," he murmured into her ear. "I've gotta shoot the rest of the show, but I can't wait to get you home." She thought her heartbeat increased then, if such a thing were possible, and then she was left on her own to grab some water and put a bit more clothing on while watching the rest of the show.

Sophia strutted by in eight-inch heels, and, towering over them, told them how proud she was. "Some of you came into this routine as novice dancers, and you killed it! You've learned so much, and you're going to put on such a great show tomorrow!" She took off her glasses, wiped her eyes, and stashed the glasses on a prop table near the edge of the stage. Then she swayed her way to the stage to rehearse her solo act for the show.

"Oh, Kaity!" Jenny stopped by, in sneakers rather than heels, since she was stage-managing. "I wanted to make sure you knew about the prints up front."

"The what?" Kaity asked.

"Hm, Gabe had sounded kinda mysterious while setting this up. You'd better see for yourself."

Kaity wandered into the Snapdragon lobby, which she'd bustled through only hours earlier, completely focused on nailing the routine for the dress rehearsal.

On three of the walls were three portraits of her, expanded in size and framed. Each one made her look gorgeous, sensual, and earthy. And these were just the shots that she and Gabe had done on a lark; she hadn't been able to model for him again since then due to their schedules always being booked, his with weddings and hers with rehearsals. She stepped closer to one, and saw that he had labeled it: "Persephone in repose." They'd talked about getting her in for another shoot and making the mythology content more explicit, and Kaity had mentioned that she felt drawn to the myth of Persephone, because it'd taken her six months to wake up into a new life. But this...this was perfect. Gabe's artistic eye had not only made her feel and look beautiful, but had also told part of her story.

Misty-eyed, she put on sweatpants and a Snapdragon logo hoodie she'd bought at the studio last week and wandered back into the main studio to watch the remainder of the show. Gabe was kneeling, standing, bending at all angles to capture various shots, while the other onlookers cheered and hollered for the dancers. Kaity was, once again, blown away by the skill and artistry she saw, but this time it wasn't scary to see open displays of sexuality. She didn't feel threatened by it, because there was no one in her life anymore to threaten her with it, with the imposition of a good/bad dichotomy onto women who used sexual displays to please men vs. those who did it for their own enjoyment. And this time, she could start to identify some of the pole moves and dance moves she was seeing, and the sense of pride and accomplishment had her jostling Anabelle and smiling at Miriam and enjoying the hell out of the show, even though it wasn't a real show for a real audience.

It's all for us, Kaity thought to herself. This dance, this way of moving the body...it was to make the dancer feel good, and her compatriots and friends. Any other good feelings were just a pleasant side effect, confident or strong or sexy feelings to be enjoyed watching tricks on YouTube or in clubs or wherever dancers thrived. The best dancers danced for themselves, and as this new puzzle piece fell into place in her mind, she resolved to infuse even more of these feelings into her performance the next night.

But first, she had to grab Gabe and tell him how wonderful he was. And maybe ravage him a little once they got home, too.

Epilogue

Gabe fist-bumped Alex as she walked into Snapdragon for the late summer showcase.

"Hey, thanks for arriving early to claim your ticket," he said. "I haven't gotten to give my comp tickets to anyone yet, so I appreciate it."

"No problem, bro," Alex replied, looking around at the studio. "How was your sister's graduation?"

"It was great," Gabe said, wistfully smiling. "Now that she's starting high school, I get to volunteer at her school's photography club, so my stepmom has upped my visits to the house."

"Awesome. And what did you want to ask me...?"

Gabe pulled Alex aside. None of the other audience members had arrived yet, but there were dancers walking in and out of the various studios in various states of undress, and Gabe didn't know which of them knew Kaity.

"Okay, look, she told me she loved me two months ago, a little after the showcase where she performed," Gabe whispered. "I of course said it back. I need to know if it's too soon to propose."

Alex furrowed her brow, but then her eyes lost focus as another gorgeous dancer strode by, wearing tall leopard-print heels and a short silk robe.

"I, uh...I think it's fine so long as you specify that it's a long engagement, since her divorce was, like, almost a year ago."

"All right, I can work with that," Gabe stated. "We're not living together just yet, but we've been talking about it."

"Talking about what?" Kaity asked, walking into the studio. She greeted Alex with a hug and Gabe with a kiss.

"Living together," Gabe said smoothly, cautioning Alex to shut up with a stern look. Alex just nodded.

"Oh, that...I think we'll figure it out," Kaity said with a smile. "I like my place but it'd be really nice to have more space at home to practice dance. Maybe even put a pole up." She gave Gabe another kiss. "You're working...I'll find a seat and let you be. It'll be nice to be in the audience this time."

"I think you're on solid ground," Alex said to Gabe after Kaity had walked into the main studio.

"I know, man, I know," Gabe replied. He wasn't sure who felt luckier, him or Kaity, but as long as they each kept feeling that way, he figured they'd be good. How he had lucked into finding someone who was good for him, even as she was finding herself at the same time, was beyond him...but he was happy that things had worked out that way.

There were more backstage photos to capture, but Gabe darted into the main room anyway, to give Kaity another kiss or three. Her smile grew, and he shared one of his own, and with his lips quickly brushing hers, he tried and failed to remember the last time that he'd felt so happy. And the best part was that they were still growing, and growing together.

THE END

Want more pole dance romance? Join my mailing list at http://jjsommerswrites.com

Stay tuned for the next book, which follows Miriam when she lands in an enemies-to-lovers situation. An excerpt follows.

Preview of Miriam's Mismatch

"**L**ook at this!" a guy guffawed.

"Holy shit," a second responded with a chortle. "Looks like we know where to find all the sluts," said the third as he strode into the classroom.

Miriam's head snapped up, her black ponytail flying. She had just posted a flyer advertising pole classes at Snapdragon on the corkboard outside the room. This was the last classroom she would have to set foot in as an undergraduate, and it was already promising to be hell.

As the final speaker walked in, Miriam stared daggers at him, and he didn't even seem to see her. Her heart pounded a furious thud as she took in his blond Ivy League haircut, slate gray eyes, and tall, muscular frame. Of course he was in a polo shirt. Fucking of course.

His two friends followed, and Miriam dubbed them Slick Back and Fade Buzz after their respective hairstyles. They also wore polo shirts.

She'd known this was a risk, that advertising for her beloved pole dance classes could attract ignorant comments. But damn if knowing it and experiencing it weren't totally different things.

As the three polo stooges sat together at the back of the room, another few students trickled in. Mechanical pencils clicked. Notebooks were opened. The room vibrated with sick tension, the fear of a hellish summer hanging over all their heads.

Still, there were just over a dozen students inside the classroom; they were racially diverse and most, like Miriam, looked to be in their mid to late twenties, since this was a commuter school in the heart of metropolitan Mariontown.

And it was a summer session, which meant an intense schedule.

And it was statistics.

It was the last class Miriam needed to graduate with her community psychology Bachelor's degree. Of course she'd put it off, like most people she knew had, no matter what their degree was in. Pulling out a notebook, she hoped that the professor wouldn't be a complete hard-ass and would understand that most students were in this just to knock out the requirement and pass.

The instructor walked in and started setting up at the computer console. Miriam scoped the teacher out: white woman, probably in her fifties, short wavy hair, business suit. Hopefully those were all good signs of a teacher who took her subject matter seriously but would still try to help students when they needed it.

Miriam could still hear the guys talking, though. She turned around and saw Ivy League getting out a notebook, while Slick Back and Fade Buzz continued to jibe each other.

"I wonder if any of those bitches dance at the local clubs," Slick Back was saying, loudly as if he didn't care who heard.

"They could dance on *my* pole anytime," Fade Buzz chortled.

Miriam's skin burned. She tried out words in her head, found them lacking. Her lips pulled so tautly in a frown, she could feel her deep green lipstick stretching into flakes.

Right then the professor started talking, and thankfully the guys behind her shut up. Apparently even these turds couldn't risk failing summer stats.

Syllabus day went about as expected. It was an accelerated schedule due to it being a summer class, so they had a lesson plan to get through in addition to learning the structure and expectations of the course. Luckily it was mostly about the distinction between qualitative and quantitative data, which as a psych major, Miriam was already familiar with.

As she took some basic notes, Miriam crossed and uncrossed her legs. She heard a snicker behind her, wondered if it was aimed at her. She knew her plaid miniskirt showed off a decent amount of leg, and most of her tattoos as well. That thought made her sigh: no new ink for a while, not until she could figure out where to place a tattoo so that it wouldn't get banged up on the pole while healing. At least she'd gotten the Baba Yaga hut, a cottage walking on chicken legs that extended their scaly claws down to her right knee, before getting into pole dance.

Another whisper. Miriam refused to turn around and look. Most dudes had things to say about her tattoos, things she was definitely not interested in hearing.

The professor, Dr. Jessica Mayer, ended with an overview of the major assignments of the class, emphasizing that they had to begin their group projects now in order to have enough time to finish them by the session's end.

Group work...Miriam shuddered. That had been one of her least favorite things about being in school so long, graduating first with a bachelor's in biology and now being most of the way to her community psychology degree. When she was with people in her major, it was fine. When she'd done that slinky choreography with Kaity and Anabelle, plus Nina, Leanne, and Mo, that was fine. They all wanted to be there, and they'd all committed to make that happen.

Not so much in the gen ed classes Miriam had taken in college. Intro to sociology had been a particular horror show, with eight people assigned to a group and half of them being no-shows for most of the semester. She refused to let some slackers drive down her grade, because it was on her to make it in college and in her hopeful profession as an art therapist.

Luckily, this one sounded like it wouldn't be too bad. Students would work in pairs to apply some statistical theories out in the real world. Open-ended projects were good, Miriam mused. She could work with those kinds of guidelines.

...but they were being assigned partners. That was potentially very bad. Miriam drummed her black-painted nails on her desk, not caring if they chipped. She had to trim her nails before her next pole class anyway, since she hadn't yet mastered the ninja skills of the women with long nails or acrylics who somehow didn't break them while death-gripping a pole to do athletic things off the ground.

Dr. Mayer took this as an opportunity to call roll, reminding everyone that she had a strict attendance policy because this was an intense class where

participation counted. Any other day, Miriam would've nodded approvingly, not caring if that marked her as a dork or a teacher's pet. She knew she learned best by showing up and doing the work.

But on this day, Miriam stayed still, loosening her posture so she could easily swivel her head and see the three polo stooges as they were identified.

Slick Back: Shinu Nair.

Fade Buzz: Aiden Smith.

Ivy League: Lucas Trevasino.

Miriam raised her hand when Dr. Mayer called her full name, Miriam Weiss, and then she went back to staring at the front of the room so that she didn't give the jerks behind her any of the attention they so clearly craved.

It was getting close to the end of the hour, and Dr. Mayer had promised they'd only meet for an hour on the first day of class, though the class technically met for two hours. Miriam respected that level of integrity, so she fought not to start fidgeting and packing her things, as eager as she was to get out of there.

It was Monday, so she had pole class with Anabelle and Kaity, so that at least was something to look forward to.

"Before I let you go," Dr. Mayer said, "I'd like to put you in your project groups so you can get started on those. I'll read aloud the assigned pairs, let you find each other, and then we can call it a day."

Miriam sat stock-still as she listened to the first few pairs being called. There were under twenty people in the class, so it wouldn't be a long wait to know how her summer would go based on this assignment.

Four pairs were called. Then five. Miriam didn't know anyone else in the class, so she didn't know who was getting saved and who was getting screwed.

Dr. Mayer kept talking. "The next pair is Miriam Weiss," and Miriam sat up straighter at this, "and Lucas Trevasino."

Slowly, tension freezing her body, Miriam turned in her seat to stare at Ivy League. He stared back at her, his hair immaculate and his gray eyes unreadable. Miriam made sure that her face was expressionless, her green lips a neutral line. It was how she interacted with the world, how her family in general interacted with the world: if they don't know who you are, what you truly want, then they can't hurt you.

The instructor stated that class was officially over, and encouraged the new pairs to exchange contact information.

Lucas looked down, breaking off the stare, but then he got up and started walking towards Miriam.

Well, shit.

...to be continued.

Acknowledgments

So many people helped make this novel idea a reality! I'm so grateful to all my writer friends who offered advice and assistance at various stages of this project. And of course to all my Chromies for being such amazing dance friends, teachers, and colleagues.

Thanks go to Donna Martz of Martzproofing.com for the stellar job with the manuscript, and to Fiona Jayde Media for the gorgeous cover.

My mom and sister were my first readers, and their encouragement kept me going even when revisions seemed too daunting. My three early readers Meli, Jessica, and Lucy gave me great feedback on areas for improvement.

About the Author

J.J. Sommers is a dancer and author who resides in the Midwest. When not writing, she is probably dancing, and vice versa. She loves jade splits and hates elbow stands.

Her website is:
http://jjsommerswrites.com

You can connect with her on Facebook:
https://www.facebook.com/jjsommersauthor

And Instagram:
https://www.instagram.com/j.j.sommers/